ISLA RISING

Isla Rising

A Tale of Love, Death and Destiny

P.J. JOHNSON

Ferguson Books

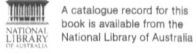 A catalogue record for this book is available from the National Library of Australia

ISBN: 9780645268508 (Paperback)
ISBN: 9780645268515 (Ebook)

Printed & Channel Distribution: Lightning Source | Ingram (USA/UK/EUROPE/AUS)
Cover Artwork & Design—Laila Savolainen, Pickawoowoo Publishing Group
Interior Formatting—Pickawoowoo Publishing Group
Editor—Michèle Drouart

Publisher—Ferguson Books

To Jessie and Sam
with thanks

Light thickens, and the crow
makes wing to th' rooky wood
- Macbeth Act III scene 2
William Shakespeare

For those who love with heart and soul
there is no separation
- Rumi

Under the wide and starry sky,
Dig the grave and let me lie.
Glad did I live and gladly die,
And I laid me down with a will.
This be the verse you grave for me:
Here he lies where he longed to be;
Home is the sailor, home from sea,
And the hunter home from the hill.
- Robert Louis Stevenson
Epitaph on his grave in Vailima on Samoa

SAMAIN IS A LIMINAL TIME BETWEEN THE
DEATH OF SUMMER AND THE BIRTH OF WINTER,
WHEN THE THRESHOLD OF THE OTHER WORLD IS
NEARER TO THIS WORLD — A TIME THAT IS OUT-
SIDE OF ORDINARY TIME.

Edinburgh, Scotland 23 October
1833

Isla's narrative

I am dying; I know it well enough. It does not matter that Dr. Walters comes up from Little France to tell me my heart is beating like a drum, that I will live for another year, mebbe two. Or that Charlotte is full of pretty lies of how well I look, and how much better I seem. I have the inside knowledge; I will go soon. I am ready enough to go, to surrender my soul and be done with all this. Lately I have longed for it. But there is still one thing that I must do before I move on to the darkness and the mystery.

Slowly I readjust my blankets. The doctor has just left and now I pray. I am old, very old, so old that I don't really know how old I am. On that score and what day it is, or where I put my glass down I am very vague. My skin is wrinkled and spotted and my grey hair is streaked with white, although I pretend that it is not. I am quite sick of being abed, but my body is useless. This old body; it can find no way to lie that doesn't pain me. Now it's cold, now it's hot, it can't keep its food down, it's always tired. This body used to be my servant but now it is my master. But that is only my body; my brain is as braw as ever, and I enjoy a laugh. Aye, on some subjects I'm sharp as a needle. I know everyone who visits (though I may forget their name); I know the news of the day, who is who in politics and the Kirk. And today there is something that I want to do.

These days my heart beats irregular but the heart feelings are still there. My eyes do gleam when Hannah, or anyone else, mentions my Dunc, though it's years since he passed. Ah, he were a grand man, a proper man, though times I were devil to him.

I run my fingers along Belle's spine, feeling each wee bump, making her purr with pleasure. Ever since I've been abed I have had a long pinch of time to study my fine, striking tabby. The triangle of her nose is red as berries, her chin is white as the snow on the heath and her slanted almond-shaped eyes are a blazing yellow, green and gold all whirled into one. Black slits of pupils watch everything and miss nothing. She has russet-coloured fur with black stripes, and two of these sooty stripes appear above the inner curve of her eyes and arc upward like the Cossack's sabres. More black stripes sit in a necklet around her throat. Och, I would know her in any crowd of tabbies. Her whiskers are long and so attuned she can sense a wee flea on the other side of the door, and her ears are always on alert. Lithe and lean and fussy she be; likes to play with mice and birds, tossing them back and forth between her paws and rolling them about on the ground. She rarely eats them but puts them away to play with later. Aye, she is a fusspot, my Belle. Her claws are like the finest needles; I could do my sewing with them. She does not take to being patted except by me and Charlotte, and now and again by Hannah; she chooses whose ankles she rubs against and whose lap she deigns to rest on, and they are not many. Aye, she may be a dumb beast, but I swear she knows more than many humans.

Belle reminds me so of Duncan; she always followed him about, sat on his lap and ate from his hand as if no one else existed. My Dunc, I'm still missing him as if he had been here this morning. He was, still is, the love of my life; his death was nearly my death too. I did not want to live no more, so desolate was I; not a thing I would ever show to the world but still I hug it to myself and bide my time. I long for him just like the lassie I was when we met. Soon, I think I will join him; soon, God will let me go. I'm not afraid nor worried. No, though I ken not what it will be like. I read the Holy Bible every day and it tells me little of Heaven; but I am sure there be a place where I will find Duncan and that place will be Heaven for me.

I lie still staring at the low ceiling; I've no energy at all for moving. I want to rise but cannot. Trapped now, forever in the bed. I am in a dream really, a long slow dream that lasts through days and nights, dreaming of Duncan and how I loved him. And he loved me too. Of how he wrapped his arms so lovingly around me and smiled that slow seductive smile. 'We're connected you and I. We've been connected ever since that day in the village, me trying to sell my strange medicines to a bonny lass.' He always spoke proper, Duncan; he wasn't *a country fool, like me. With each word my heart beat harder. Oh, he got into my soul alright but I wondered, what should I do? Deep inside I felt the same as he; that I was his, and he was mine. I knew it deep, ye ken. But I'd seen my ma slaving her life away and swore never to be as her. Yet I could not stop myself.*

I fell, like a stone, into love. How I cursed my foolishness even as I rejoiced. Love blotted out everything else; I was anxious and content all at once. Oh, so content!

Now ye know I were a bonnie lassie then — all green eyes and red hair, and I'd had my fun a teasin' all the would-be lovers round the place. I'd danced a wild round at every dance and flirted wi' them all, though I got the strap for it at home now and again. Oh, I did nay care at all. The fun was too great. And now here was this fine lad, all educated and ready to have a shop of his own, talking and bowing so grandly to me. To me! And well-dressed too, like a gentleman.

All shy I look up at him. 'I feel the same.' The words caught in my throat like burrs. I didna want to say them but out they came and how his pretty eyes lit up like beacons. 'Aye, laddie,' I said more firmly. 'I feel it, it's running all through me.' His arms tightened about me; his fine, strong arms, arms that could a'been a smithy's. I could feel his heart beatin' strong right through his shirt. Wild as any maid in love, I darted forward to give him a wee peck of a kiss, aye, just on his cheek, mind. His eyes closed an' his breathing stopped, I swear. I put my hand to his head and messed up his bonnie black hair . . . slipped through his arms and ran quick away trying hard to stop giggling with happiness.

Oh, he chases me then all over the hard hillock until he lands me and lifts me up. He swings me round and round and us all lit by the sun and the air full of the buzzing of bees and calls of birds. Och, such bliss it is. We walk together holding hands and now and then sharing a kiss; nothing matters more than that. He pours out strength; I take it from him like a bee drawing nectar from the flower. Here, I thinks, is what God had made me for. Duncan! I am where I want to be, where I need to be, have to be, right here in his arms. Here I am, in love, and I am not gonna let any soul take that away.

I lifted my face to his and I drank deep of those fine, braw kisses just like wine that only left me wanting more. His hands so warm, so well set into mine.

And now I am nothing but a dry old stick that Hannah watches with that bonny smile on her face, making me wonder what she is thinking of. My servant for over thirty years, she knows me inside out, backwards and upside down too. She is my friend as well servant; she knows each wrinkle and the verra day my hair went to grey. Her own hair has gone grey now and she moves slow like there's a load on her back. Aye, she is a faithful one, there in her clean white apron. Yawning as she sits at my bedside, her eyes slowly close; I will bide for a while, dream of Duncan and let her rest.

I hear the front door creak open and the bell tinkle; the door shuts slowly and closes with a dull thud, then light footsteps come running up the stairs. Hannah's eyes go a searching for mine; I give her a wink and turn my head a wee bit so I see young Charlotte as she comes in, all flushed and bright. Belle lifts her head to see and lowers it on my bed again. Och, she is a right lazy lass, my Belle.

Charlotte's dark hair is blown back and shows her fine fair skin that has a faint sheen on it from hurrying so. Her eyes flash with extra clear whites around glowing black centres.

'Hello grandmother,' she says, giving me a wee peck on the forehead. 'Shall I sit with you for a while?' She looks worried in spite of all her bright smiles. Aye, she shall never be good at the cards, my Charlotte, not the way her face changes as she talks, so full of her feelings — I could watch her forever.

'Aye, my chick.' My voice comes out so hoarse that I croak like a frog. I hold out these old arms and she hugs me close.

'Dr. Walters has just left,' I add.

Hannah, looking at Charlotte over the top of my grey hairs, gives a most tiny shake of her head. Oh, I kin see her alright, though they think I cannot. 'I will make ye some tea,' she says and goes out through the open door.

'I dinna pass the doctor.' Charlotte clings to my hands giving them wee kisses and looking up into my tired eyes with her fresh young ones. 'What did he say?'

'Och, the same old thing! Tells me to rest. He sees to my comfort, clever man that he be, and puts a drop of whiskey in the tea that Hannah brings.' I chuckle, but this time it comes out soft and weak.

With Charlotte here beside me, I think, now is the time to put my scheme into place. Putting my left hand into my right, I commence a'tugging at my wedding ring and trying to twist it off my finger.

This seems to disturb Belle and she, spoilt animal that she is, jumps off the bed and wanders away, swishing her tail and looking back at me over her shoulder as she goes. Haughty as always.

'What are you doing, grandma?' Charlotte asks me.

'I want these rings off; but they have been there so long now, they are nearly grown into my finger,' I say. 'Get me some ointment, my darlin, will you?'

Belle's narrative

It is time for me to take over the telling of this tale now. Grand as she is, Isla is getting old and canna tell it at all sensibly. Nor could any of them. But I can. You see, I can go all sorts of places they cannot and find out things they would never even know -- and no one pays any attention at all. We cats do not matter — we barely count. People assume we can't hear or think. But we can. Och, how wrong they are. Now see how sharpish I am out of the sickroom and following this chit of a gel down the stairs. She is into the shop and up to the counter in no time at all and I have to admit, she is a bonny-looking lass as she stands there chatting away with John. Another silly bugger, who does not know yet that he is born. She only has to look his

way and he flushes red all over, and well aware of it
she is!

'Can I have some ointment, Mr. Muir, to rub on
Grandma's hands?'

Well, of course he can't look at her and can only
mumble a reply, and out the back he goes like a scared
rabbit. I go too, to watch him as he fiddles and farts
about. I know well that he likes it out the back much
better than at the front. He is full too shy and self-
conscious there, when now in the back amongst the
rows of bottles and potions, he begins to recover and
know his stuff. I curl up in the corner and wait, and
he pays me no heed. The room is still set up just
as Duncan had it. A very particular man Duncan was
about his apothecary's shop. It is full of shelves and
cubicles, all carefully labelled. At the back herbs grow
in pots, and on the fire a smelly something is being
heated. It is just as it should be; Mr. Muir hasn't
moved anything at all, not one iota. They were a grand
team, Duncan and Mr. Muir, aye, working together like
a couple of brothers with no rancour between them.
He has the ointment in his hands but is not moving.
Frozen, like a statue, too nervous to return, but finally
we go through the door together, and he hands the jar
to Charlotte.

'Will that do?"

'Well, it'll have to do, I suppose.' The chit is never
really kind to Mr. Muir. She finds him stuffy and
pedantic, is my guess. She does not like his earnest-
ness, his young awkwardness or his tongue-tied

speech, nothing at all like her Luke's easy manner. And the more fool her, I say.

Isla's narrative

Charlotte takes my hand, rubs lanolin all around my finger, making the ointment melt, working it in and around my rings, and warming my cold flesh as it releases a faint odour of sheep fat. Her dark locks falling forward as she bends over my hand are a grand sight. It is the fine thick black hair of my Duncan that she has, aye that it is. She gently rubs the finger until at last the ring rotates easily. I take hold of it and bring it to the middle joint; past that it will not budge. I bring it forward again and again. Charlotte looks anxious, but finally it passes right over the knuckle and off my finger.

'What a struggle!' I smile at the child as I place it carefully onto the coverlet and begin again the same process with my engagement ring.

'It was a bonnie day when your Granddad bought me this ring. He let me choose just as I wanted, and I liked this garnet fine, so strong and full the colour is, d'ye see? It seemed full of fire . . . still does. I remember just how it was - him with his serious face and me trying so hard to be serious with him. And yet I had the idea to pretend I'd changed my mind, just to tease him a wee bit.'

Charlotte laughs at the thought of us old people being young. I wager she canna even imagine it.

I make a face as the second ring sticks on the joint

just as the first did. 'Och but I could-na' do it, not with his eyes on me, so fond and so dear. The mischief went straight out of me. Aye, lassies may be foolish things, ye ken.' I work on more lanolin and enjoy the feel of its warmth and its greasy texture sinking into my thin skin.

'Aye, yet I'll wager ye led him a merry dance,' she says. 'I remember his tales well enough. But now dinna worry any more, grandma. Why can't the ring stay on your finger? Keep it there and stop hurting yourself.'

I tug and pull until the garnet comes off with a rush and almost flies from my hand. 'Och,' I says. 'That was a battle fit for Napoleon.' I work at the poor joint for a while, trying to get the blood to flow again. Then I push the plain gold band back on. It is not so hard this time, but the finger is red and sore, and I massage it with my thumb, grateful for the lanolin. I need a couple of deep breaths before I speak again.

'Charlotte, I want you to have this,' I say, picking up her hand and placing the garnet onto her palm. 'It's never been off my finger, not since the day it went on, until today.' I give a dry chuckle. 'You can use it for your own engagement ring if you like, or not, just as you please.'

Her face changes, softens a wee bit, looking at me.

The shop bell tinkles; the bustle of someone arriving and a murmur of voices rise up to us.

'Duncan would be glad to see the shop still so busy these days. Ah, don't cry, child. All goes on, as it should. Would you ask me to live forever?' I can hear my voice quaver. 'There, there . . . you will have us both with *you now, Duncan and I. We will always be here' — I tap Charlotte's hand — 'in the ring.'*

'Thank you,' says Charlotte in a whisper.

I wonder if she will ever marry; if she will be as happy as I was. I take the ring and slide it onto the ring finger of her right hand. We both stare at it, I at the smooth fresh skin it now rests on, such a contrast my own.

'I will take care of it,' she says. 'Good care.'

'That's my girl,' I say, my voice unintentionally harsh, like the cackling of the chickens. I canna seem to control it these days.

I feel verra tired now, tired of talking. I hear the clink and rattle of tea things. Here's Hannah and I push my hand, with the finger that's now so red and sore, under the pillow and pull out my metal flask. It's battered but full of fine old whisky, a lot like me. In a different voice again I croak, 'let's have that tea, Hannah.'

Belle's narrative

They do not think of me, that I may like a little titbit. I think I shall have to get out of here now; they will only chat and Isla will drift off to sleep. There are times when it's just too boring for such a lively eye as mine. I have my favourite haunts and those I don't like at all, but feel I should keep a watch on for the sake of the populace. Most places don't mind a wee visit from one of my persuasion, and in fact, we are usually quite welcome as we keep the mice away. The place I am going to is not a comfortable lair for me but out of loyalty to my mistress I will check on it. There they are all liars and thieves, it seems to me, although some of the other poor miserable humans I know don't ken at all that they are. They *say* they are a solicitor's office, but listen to this offal, meant to be conversation.

Here is Charels, a barrel of a man. At first he can do nothing better than grunt. Then he starts bellowing. It is all very unpleasant.

'Where's Silver? Silver!'

'Aye, Mr. Charels, sir.' A young, somewhat dishevelled fellow comes in from the rear of the office.

'Put that fire out, lad. We don't need it yet. We're not made of money, you fool.'

'Hold on, Silver,' says Luke Harker. 'We do have a couple of clients coming in soon. It might be better to have the fire going.'

Again Charels grunts. (He grunts a lot.) 'All right . . . appearances! I know.' Charels shoos Silver away with his hand, worse than if he was a cat. 'But I won't last much longer if word doesn't come soon.'

'It won't be for much longer.'

'How do ye know? It may all go awry yet.'

'It won't; it's nearly over. Just stay strong a bit longer. I've staked my whole life on this, as you know well enough. Now sit down, Charels. I'll get Silver to bring you some tea.'

Now I ask you, what are these precious villains about? It is clear that they are up to no good. And it matters, you see, because this Luke is Charlotte's

Luke, and Charlotte is my mistress's good grandchild. So I listen and watch and meow occasionally, just to seem as usual. I pretend to look for a mouse, but all the time I am on a very different type of surveillance.

In the door there comes a perfectly horrible woman, a dreadful Mrs. McIver, who hates me. And how Luke's tone changes, all oily now.

'Good afternoon, Mrs. McIver. How grand it is to see you! Come in out of the cold. Here, sit by the fire,' he says, moving the usual visitor's chair closer to the warming flames. He is all attention. 'What can we do for you? Would you like some tea? You must be very chilled.' He gives her a look of great concern; she doesn't feel cold because she rejoices in being a warm-blooded woman with plenty of fat; but his look convinces her she is a highly desirable and helpless female who needs to be taken care of. She melts into his look and nods, as he conducts her to the chair and calls Silver with quite a sharp urgency. The order for tea is given.

I know what will happen now; things will become more and more tiresome, so I leap up onto the window ledge and fuss and fidget until they let me out.

I wander around for a wee while, and after a time I meet a couple of mates and we sit together in the sun, gossiping and drowsing, and sometimes have a wee play fight. After the sun sets they head off and I go right home for my dinner, and maybe a saucer of cream if I am lucky. And who's to say what will fall to the floor. Hannah is right canny but she knows what a good mouser I am. And so I am, not a mouse to be found in my house, no, nor the shop either. After eating I fall to being bored again so off I go to see what I can see -- for night time is the right time for cats. I trek along until I come to Calton Burial Ground; I like it here. It's usually peaceful, and sometimes I sit on a headstone and watch the comings and goings of the old spirits who hang about, unable to move on. But tonight there is a light, and a sound of clanging like Highland claymores taking part in a sword fight, not a great din but a distinct one, and I hurry to spy on what is going on.

Here are a couple of lads I know, grave robbers they are. One, in torn and ragged clothes, digs, while the other, Crowe, who is a deal taller, keeps a lookout.

'Hurry, Tom!' urges Crowe, holding a lantern above the grave.

Tom hurries.

Crowe is dark - with dark eyes and black-hair - and as menacing as the crow he is named for. If he was a crow I could catch and eat him. He looks warily around, but keeps an eye on his partner, who is not to be trusted, not ever. Tom's ears stand out like jug handles, and his poor dim eyes reflect the light from the lantern. The burial ground is a lonely place for them, lonely and frightening, even for Crowe, however hard he pretends to be a brave one. And the night is black as pitch; I wonder, have they picked it for its very blackness? . . . because without moonlight, the watcher in the tower will not see them, unless they are very unlucky.

Tom grunts and digs until he hears a thud, whereat he giggles like a child.

'Shh.' In the dark, Crowe scowls. He jumps down and begins to scrape away the dirt with his hands.

They do not lift out the coffin but wrestle off the heavy lid; inside, it is painted with gold and silver stars. They do not notice me there, watching. No, they are in too much of a rush. Now comes the nasty part. They lift up the body, not yet light but stiff as a plank and place it in the barrow they have brought. Some of the spirits have gathered round now; they do not like grave robbers and watch with expressions of great Gaelic disapproval. At Tom's feet a creature slithers past. The air around us vibrates as a tawny owl swoops down. 'Too woo, too woo,' it calls. Tom lets out a cry. He does not like the burial ground with its dark plots and atmosphere of dread. He goes there only to please Crowe, who looks after him and whom he idolises. Crowe is his father and his mother and Tom will do as he wishes, whether he hates it or not. He digs for Crowe and as he digs, he closes his mind to every-thing else. I do not dislike Tom, but Crowe, ugh! How he does pull the wee mannie's strings. I cannot say he does not look after Tom, because he does, but he does not always treat him well. To be sure, they have no home, no work, no money and they only do this to eat. It makes it hard for me, scavenger as I am, to feel too harsh about them. The spirits have no such reservations and begin to move about, letting off that feeling of menace that they are so good at. The two men shove the coffin lid back on, fill in the grave, and get away as quick as ever they can. They meet no one, only a thin and dirty grey cat that stares at them in silence before bolting with a yowl over a low stonewall. It is only Moony, who is, I know well, as harmless as a butterfly on the breeze. I consider and decide to follow them, for I ken where they are going and I like to keep an eye on such enterprises as theirs. To the east a cold wind springs up and rain mists down; it will soak them through before they get far.

It is a bit of distance to Little France Crescent and the Royal Infirmary where Dr. Walters lives, so I run up past them and jump up onto the barrow with an elegant leap — I am less afraid of the dead than of getting wet — and settle down for the ride. Perhaps I am a bit lazy as well. Anyway, they do not even see me in the dark. The wind and the rain increase and I hide from it as best I can, hating the horrible wetness of it all. It is past midnight by the time we arrive and the doctor is half asleep, dozing by his fire and his whiskey bottle. I can see him clear enough through the window and get down ready for the opening of the door. Crowe taps lightly and the doctor wakes and rises. He opens the heavy oak door to the two scarecrows that wait on his doorstep, the handcart and its grisly burden in the shadows behind them.

'Doctor?' Crowe whispers.

'Come in.' Dr. Walters nods. Miscreants such as

these are his mainstay, poor human. The whiskey is for his guilt and shame but the man is driven. They bring the corpses that are his drug, and he always needs more, as many as they can bring. Still, they are never enough, never will be until he finds his cures. Tom gently lifts the body in its muddy blue dress from the cart and enters the room. He lays it, still dripping from the rain, onto a long table cleared for the purpose. Silently, Crowe collects their money from the sideboard where it waits for them. Tom giggles, but stops at a glare from Crowe.

After they have left, Dr. Walters stands and stares at the body, torn between his conscience and his distaste. He pours himself another drink.

'Stop your havering, man, it's late enough already,' he mutters to himself, trying to still his shaking hands as he begins unbuttoning the high-necked dress. 'I beg your pardon, lassie.' He nods solemnly. 'It has to be done.' I stay and watch. Do not think I am ghoulish; it is the doctor that I worry about and think it is better for him not to be completely alone at this time. I rub against his leg, purring, surely to him a sign of life.

24 October

Isa's narrative

The frightened faces of Charlotte and Hannah peer down at me. I try to lift my heavy head, but it will nay budge an inch. My breath is a wheeze, strange and ragged. I feel my body falling to pieces.

Me and Dunc on the Waters of Leith, him rowing and me chattering away.

'I'll not share ye, not even with the good Lord,' he says .

I reach over and touch his face. He fumbles, and in trying to take my hand in his, he drops the oar with a splash. Over the side he goes and into the cold water. I am annoyed and worried in the same moment. I canna swim and, left alone, I feel abandoned by the man. The boat rocks alarmingly so that I have to hold on tight to avoid going in myself; and then Dunc's grinning face appears before me dripping wet, and with a hint of mischief in his snapping black eyes. With his strong hands he rocks the skiff even harder until, terrified, I am tipped right in. He catches me and holds me to him, and plants a kiss on my lips. 'I'll not let anything happen to ye,' he says before we both sink. The water is murky and cool, but his body is warm in my arms. My fear disappears as I know we will rise. We are tight together; it is heavenly. And then he is gone.

I look down at my bed, at the body lying in it — my old body, sure enough. My eyes are fixed and staring. I feel shocked to see it, so strange it seems, not like me at all; aye, and I am confused too, but not afraid. 'Charlotte? Hannah?' I call. Those two are looking at each other. 'Do ye hear me?'

Bending over the bed, they hide from my sight by flapping their hands, and making soft empty noises like a couple of bewildered bairns. I know it is me under the bright covers — it can be no other — but I am up here as well. How strange it seems! Am I dead? I must be, aye. I am a little surprised to find that the thought pleases me. I try to think; it is impossible. There is only feeling, and I am felled by a vast peace.

'Grandmother?' Charlotte's voice, doubtful, disbelieving, shocks me with its urgency. 'Grandmother!' she shouts, shaking me by the shoulders. I see, but cannot feel, her touch. She moves her hand to where my heart should beat, aye, where it always beat right fierce, and tilts her head close over my lips. She gasps and a tear springs to her eye, but what am I to do? Oh, I am in a right taking! They are so frightened, but I canna comfort them. There is only my old body for them to see, that lies so still and dead. Charlotte's eyes go to Hannah's; then her knees give way and she falls onto the bed. Och, my poor chick, my darling lass. Her tears begin to fall in earnest and Hannah takes her in her arms. I see it all happen, just like in a play.

'Dinna cry for me; I'm here, I'm right here beside you,' I say loudly. 'Dinna cry, my bonnie ones, hush now.' Useless. I can do nothing but watch as Hannah helps Charlotte to her chair and lets her rest her head on her shoulder. She rocks my own darling granddaughter back and forth like a wee babe. Strands of her greying hair fall over Charlotte, as if protecting her. Hannah, looking half dead herself, stares at my body; then it seems as if she holds herself straighter and settles her face. It sinks in that they cannot hear me, but I keep

trying, hoping they can sense a wee bit of the feeling, of the idea, that I am alright.

'There, there, don't ye fret. All is as it should be,' Hannah whispers, the verra words I said yesterday. I see Charlotte flinch, but her weeping slows as she tries to believe the words. Hannah rises and gently closes my eyes. It is so odd; I canna get the hang of things. I'm up here and there is me on the bed, too. It will take some getting used to for all of us. Hannah brings out a bottle of whiskey and pours a couple of stiff drinks into the glasses that are always ready on the bureau. 'Here now, a wee dram is what you need.' That's right, I think. She hands Charlotte a brimming glassful and watches until she has emptied it, then drinks her own. 'I'll go down and make some sweet tea and send for the doctor,' she says. 'Will ye nay come wi' me?'

Charlotte's delicate features contract; she adjusts her fine lace collar. 'Will I . . . what? . . . ' her voice disappears into a whisper. 'No. No, I will stay here.' She looks up into Hannah's eyes. 'Aye, I'll be fine right here, Hannah. I want to stay with Grandma. You go down and make the tea,' she says in a louder voice, giving Hannah's hand a tug. Och, that's my brave lassie. 'Go on.'

If only I could comfort them! All my pain is gone, aye and that is grand, but I want to let them know, I hate to see them so sad and solemn. How to think or what to do I do not know. What am I even capable of? Still, I feel very calm, if wanting guidance. I begin to recite the Lord's Prayer, but stop midway and look around for Duncan. Surely he should be here to meet me! 'Dun-

can! Duncan,' I cry to the ether. 'Come to me now.' Aye, where is the man? Where is he now that I need him? Why is he not here to meet me?

Belle's narrative

It was quite an adventure last night and now I am tired from my gallivanting; I spend the morning sleeping with my mistress, even though 'tis certain she is gone. I am right glad to be on the foot of her bed again, like always, if only Hannah and Charlotte would stop flapping around like a couple of old hens. I know that Isla is well; it's simply too bad that they do not. After a while I grow tired of their fussing and go down the stairs to look for food, and — having found but little — I decide to go and search for more. I scoot out the door when a customer comes in and in a flash am off to the pub, always a good spot to pick up titbits and gossip.

I can well understand what humans find so appealing about a pub; it's warm, there's food, you can stay there all day and night if you keep drinking that appalling stuff they serve from behind the bar. Once, when I was just a wee kitten, for a joke, one of the men gave me a bowlful of ale; well, I was as sick as a dog and ye know how felines feel about canines, but it almost made me feel sorry for the poor brutes.

Now the Thistle is not a bad pub, but at the moment there are only a few patrons and soon I recognize my mates from last night. That's Tom and Crowe at the table by the window. They're drinking and sitting there looking kind of dazed and stupid, with the remains of a couple of mutton dinners in front of them. Who can blame them, after their horrible night? And maybe they will feed me a wee scrap or two of yon mutton.

Well, outside the wind howls and inside the fire burns. A couple of old men with nothing to do but gossip huddle there and talk in low, raspy tones. I am just heading for the fireplace when the door opens and a tall thin miscreant is propelled by the wind into the room. He pushes back the red hair that has been blown into a wild jumble across his face. Looking around, he spots Tom and Crowe and heads for their table. He nods to the publican who goes without hurry to the bar to pour him a glass of ale. Tom and Crowe watch as without a word the man sits down with them. I change direction and hurry over to hear what is said, for red hair has a bit of a reputation in Edinburgh.

'Sandy.' Crowe nods a greeting.

'Crowe.' Sandy nods. 'Tom, how do ye fare?' His voice, low and cautious, matches his dour expression. His damp hair flops forward, dank and bright over the sharp freckled features of his face.

Tom grins. 'Want to play dominoes, Sandy?'

Sandy ignores him. He looks carefully around the room before he speaks again, still addressing Crowe. 'Have ye anything for me?'

'No,' answers Crowe; there is a tight edge in his voice.

At the same time Tom says eagerly, 'I'll get ye something, Sandy. I will.' His simple face with its two beaming guileless eyes contorts with the effort to please.

Crowe smiles thinly.

Sandy, too, smiles, but broadly, and turns to Tom. The freckles on his face seem darker. 'Good man, Tom! There'll be shillings in it for you, to woo the bonnie lassies, aye that there will be.'

Tom half giggles, half chokes, but ducks his head and stares down at the table when he feels Crowe's dark look on him.

Slowly slewing his eyes around to Red Sandy, Crowe gives him a bleakly antagonistic glare, a 'get yer great ugly carcass out of my sight' sort of look.

Sandy sighs. Rising from his seat, he swallows his ale and leaves a coin on the table. 'I'll see you again, Tom, eh?' he says. At the door ye can see him scan the street; the wind roars in and reaches the fireplace, making the flames dance. As soon as he is gone, Crowe turns to Tom and, in a low voice, begins talking nineteen to the dozen.

Now, I've tried to report that as it was said, but I don't know if ye get the terrible atmosphere that hung around the words. It's plain as day that things are not good for Tom and Crowe, but at least red hair has gone.

Isla's narrative

I decide to follow Hannah down the stairs. Perhaps I will find my Duncan in his old shop, just a waitin' for me. Perhaps he has been there all along. It's been such a long time since I've been out of my room, or indeed could move at all, that I be in a fine rare excitement, more than I can tell ye. First, I come to my own entrance hall that, since being stuck in ma bed, I have nay seen for months. Two cloaks hang on pegs and Mr. Muir's woollen plaid is on another. I like the sight of it all, bein' just the same as it always was. Any wee body coming in from the street kin go straight ahead into the shop, just as Hannah does now with me sharp behind her.

All looks tidy and clean, giving off a fine feel of welcome and a pleasant scent of lavender. It surprises me that I can smell too, as well as hear and see. Och, how it warms me to see it again! Hannah calls out for Mr. Muir, for he is nowhere to be seen. He answers straight-away, though, and comes directly through the open doorway that leads to Duncan's old herbarium at the back. He looks at her keenly, stops in his tracks. 'Has she gone then, Hannah?'

Hannah nods silently. I kin sense her still sadness, though she does not shed a tear.

'Was it peaceful?' he asks.

Ah, he's a braw lad, young Mr. Muir, and I always liked him well, him an' his eager eyes.

'Aye, peaceful enow. Will ye go for Dr. Walters, Mr.

Muir? And mayhap Pastor Furphy too? Yon lassie could bear with some comforting, I reckon.' Hannah tries to smile but the words pour out of her in a raw, cheerless way. 'And so could I.'

'As ye wish,' he says. 'I will miss her too, Hannah.' Without any fuss, he takes off his apron and wraps his plaid around him. He turns the sign hanging on the door from 'open' to 'closed' and hurries out into the watery sunshine.

I spy round for my Duncan; he's not in the shop at all. 'Well, he always was a wee bit tardy for things,' I say to myself. There is much in the shop that has changed, and it serves to distract me. Mr. Muir has moved the sweetie basket for the wee bairns farther back on the counter. 'Humph,' I mutter. 'They won't be able to reach it, the mean thing.'

Hannah goes on to the kitchen and begins making the tea; I float in behind her, and blow a kiss to Belle who is licking her paws while she suns herself at ease on the windowsill. She turns her head and opens up those wild green and gold eyes to stare in my direction. Och, I believe she can see me. I make a face at her.

'How about ye, Belle? Ye can see me, can ye not? And can ye hear me?' I cry, and Belle just stares at me in the way of all heathen cats, without blinking or moving. But she gets up and comes over to greet me like she always did, circling my feet.

Hahaha! Well, at least I kin still do something. If Belle knows me, I won't feel quite so lonely. And truly, if she knows me, others may too. After all, I can't be the *only spirit around the place, nor Belle the only animal that can recognize me. I am delighted, just for the comfort of her.*

Now my thoughts fly once more to Duncan. Where are ye, ma wee man? If I am here as I surely am, I'm as certain as can be that ye should be here with me. Why do ye leave me alone? I move about the room, and in my agitation, I wring my hands and wave my arms in the air. It is passing strange, that here I am in a fit of passion, right in front of Hannah who pays no heed as she is grieving for my death. Och, if only she knew!

And then something so amazing happens I can scarce believe it. It is the strangest thing. A bright spark flies from my hand. My hand, mind ye, not that I willed it nor wished it. And then another spark flies out and more sparks appear and more — more until there is a fine wild frenzy of sparks all about me. They just fly from my hand, wild, of their own free will. I do not understand and stare at my hand like it is the man in the moon come to life. So strange it is that I have to remind myself that I am dead, and things are different now.

The sparks light up the kitchen; I have never seen it so bright in here. It makes me quite light-headed. I turn to Hannah but of course she does not see a thing; she is staring at the kettle, a glisten in her eye. Poor hen! But the strange lights captivate me as they rise up to the ceiling where they sit and glow, such beauties, a pure white. I stare and stare. What could it mean? I look at my hand and wonder. I move it right in front of my eyes and examine its fine lines. I shake it and wag-

gle the fingers but now no sparks fly from it. Where did they come from? Why did they come? Is it important? Is there something I should do?

Hannah picks up the tea tray and goes out the door; I follow reluctantly, still full of wonder at the lights which I do not want to leave. I want to stay and watch the sparks that are glowing above me, but I must be there with Hannah and Charlotte. I rage at not being able to comfort them, but perhaps simply being nearby is a comfort. How am I to know? I only know I must stay with them.

Hannah checks to see that no one waits outside. The usual lots of colds and other ailments for October have kept Mr. Muir busy for weeks but no one is there now. She looks briefly into the shop; it is empty and up the stairs she goes, carefully balancing the tray. I watch and see that as she stops she settles her face into a smile again before she opens the door. What a great affection for her fills me!

'Dr. Walters will soon be here,' she says as she enters. 'Mr. Muir has gone for him.'

'It is well.' Charlotte takes the cup of tea she is offered. 'Thank you, Hannah.' Poor chick, her hands are a'shakin,' and her voice sounds weak again. 'Grandma would be putting a drop of whiskey in it, wouldn't she?'

'That she would,' Hannah agrees.

'And shall we do the same?'

Ah, aye, have a dram, and I could do with it, so I could.

Charlotte picks up my old flask and pours the last dregs of its raw cheer into their tea. She raises her cup.

'Sl'aint! To Grandma and a fine life.'

'To Isla!' They clink their cups and drink.

Ah, it is grand being dead, when ye can see the care in their eyes. I'm beginning to enjoy it, that I am.

Aye, a fine life . . . a fine life it was – and so was the whiskey. I reach out for the flask, madwoman that I am but the flask will not be lifted by the likes of me. My hand is air and fastens on air. As it closes in a fist, the unexpected happens again, just like it did in the kitchen a minute ago; sparks fly from my hand. But this time I notice that they come straight from the gold band of my wedding ring. Again, I touch my ring and again out they fly; I do it over and over and soon the room is so full of light I canna even see the walls. It is so beautiful! I canna help myself and caress the gold with my thumb. The incredible glowing light swells and overwhelms me. But I do not mind, I am full of delight. I am so happy to know whence the sparks come. My wedding ring! Will Dunc come now? I look around for him but all I see is Charlotte and Hannah sitting sad with their tea. How I wish they could see this fine show, but they have set-tled back in their chairs; it is plain enough that they are low and comfortable saying nothing. Their faces are fixed, and Charlotte wipes away her silent tears as they stare dumbly at my dead body; it must be going cold by now. I feel sorry for their grief, but as for me I am well satisfied. I delight in the wonderful glow that my ring has created. It is a grand display and now I know its se-

cret. I am right glad to be dead, and will be gladder, aye, when I am with my Dunc again.

Downstairs someone pounds on the door; Hannah rises and goes out and down the stairs. Out of the silence a grand commotion erupts, and someone comes rushin' up the stairs, calling out in a deep male voice, 'Charlotte! Charlotte!'

Who is this? Why does he run up the stairs so? What have I missed in my illness? A gentleman still in his overcoat comes stumbling, almost running, into my bedroom. Charlotte flies into his arms, her tears overflowing now. Here is a thing! He enfolds her; she so small and delicate, and he such a bear of a man that she nearly disappears entirely in his arms. The pair of sneaks! This has been kept from me.

'Luke!'

'I came as soon as I heard.'

'Oh, I canna bear the thought of it. I canna stop the tears.'

For a while there is nothing but sobs and murmurs.

So, Luke is it? Not having seen the man before I circle him, looking up and down his large frame, trying to gauge him. I peer into his eyes; eyes that are fixed on the bed. The man is light all over; his hair so blonde it is almost white, and his eyes such a light shade of blue and with lashes so pale that it sets my teeth on edge. His face and hands too are as white as a dish of salt. Still, I have to admit that he is a handsome man. I can see his charm, but he makes me uneasy; and perhaps he is large and dutiful, but he is no Duncan; aye, that is for certain.

I see at once that he is important. He matters dearly to Charlotte. Aye, I see that clear enough, but I wish that it was not so. There is something greatly amiss with him; I feel it in my bones. The room seems to have grown colder with him in it. All about him is an atmosphere, a feeling of unease. It circles around him softly, dangerously, but he knows it not. I am all attention now, afraid; I feel as if I am treading on eggshells by simply being here in the same room with him and whatever the force is that attends him. I pray for strength and courage for Charlotte and Hannah as well as for myself, for there is danger all around. Poor Luke! He may be as beautiful as an angel, he may be innocent as a babe, but all around him is something of the very devil. It is as if he stands in a pool of wickedness that laps, dangerous and beguiling, about his feet. Lord, I must save my Charlotte from this horror! What does it mean? And in this state how will I ever find out exactly what it is, or what I am to do for my chick to save her from this evil?

'Never mind, my love,' Luke says. It is a shock to hear a normal voice come from him. 'You must cry, there seems no help for it. You loved her, I know,' Luke pats her shoulder awkwardly, helplessly; he is no use to her, but she is blinded by her need and looks to him for comfort. But I can see that he is no comfort; he has no strength in him, nothing solid for her to cling to. Still cling she does! He begins to pace the room, but he is so

*big and the room so wee that he must stop and stand
and merely stare at my body on the bed. The sight must
unsettle him for his pale eyes begin to dart about. He
looks out the window. 'Someone is coming,' he says.*

Belle's narrative

'Tis evening and I'm going to visit one of my favourite
people, a little girl who has been feeling poorly for a
long, long time. She's a sweet wee bairn, and I like to
visit her, even though she's in the Royal Infirmary, not
a place that I enjoy at all. People in there are dying,
or they're too sick to move, or there are parts of them
chopped off. It's a terrible place and I have to close
my eyes as I go in the door. Flora is asleep in her bed;
she has only two possessions and they are both beside her – a picture book of animals and a doll that
her Ma knitted for her before she died. Flora has a
wee cough, and as I curl up at the foot of her bed, the
cough wakes her up and she reaches for her cup of
milk and sips. I see a drop of blood on the rim but she
wipes it away before anyone else notices. She smiles
at me so I move up and lay by her side, and try to
warm her. She is so cold that I ken she will be going
soon, poor child -- but even though she is so young,
it seems as if already she is terribly old and tired and
ready to go, and would go gladly, but for leaving her
Da all alone.

Well, see now Dr. Walters moving through the

ward, stopping by each bed and doing this or that, until he gets to us.

'Well, good evening, Flora. And how are you today?' He looks tired and worn out.

'I'm well, doctor. I feel so good I'm sure I could go home.' She suppresses a cough.

'Och! That's grand. Now, just let me listen to your heart.' He lays his head on her chest, looks into her mouth and her eyes, picks up her wrist and holds it. 'And how is Pinkus?' he asks, indicating the doll.

'He's grand, doctor, but he's as bored as can be. He does nay like it here,' says Flora. 'It is almost Samain, and he would like to be home for the bonfires.'

Dr. Walters picks up Pinkus who flops awkwardly as if he was a limp bird, and studies him intently. He holds him up to his ear. 'What's that?' he says, trying to inject some jollity into his voice. 'You want to stay another day? I think that's a good idea.'

The man is daft, of course. He canna' fool Flora — she is on to him.

'Well, Flora, you are doing well but I think you should stay here just a wee bit longer,' Dr. Walters continues, pretending not to notice her disappointment. 'Pinkus wants to stay too, don't you, Pinkus? And so, we three will keep a lookout for the spirits here in the Royal Infirmary when it is Samain.' He pauses, thinking. 'When is your father coming?'

'He may not come tonight, doctor. It is so verra cold. Everyone wants coal now and he'll be workin' till late.' She picks at the quilt and a solitary tear escapes her eye. 'I need to go home to look after my Da. He is sore missing my Ma.'

Well, she is breaking my heart now, and Dr. Walters' heart as well. I stay with her most of the evening, at least until supper time when I must go, or go hungry. But I feel so sad leaving her. It is too bad for such a sweetheart to suffer so!

When people look at cats like me, they do not appreciate that not one of them has the sort of perspective we have. They might think I am a nuisance, or I am cute, or hungry. But they should envy me my perspective as it is very important! As one of the fortunate ones, I can look at things in all sorts of ways, from the floor or from the ceiling, so to speak. From the sky, or curled up on someone's lap. And this does alter the way we understand things. For example, this night I am back at the Calton Burial Ground and from the top of the gravestone on which I perch I see that the clear sky allows the moon to cast its bright light onto the black iron railings, the granite headstones, the overturned turf and the unkempt grass between the plots. Tonight even I feel it as the wind blows cold — but the fantastical spirits do not feel it as they wonder if they will be released this year. It is to be soon, Samain, the regular death of summer and birth of winter cold and sea frets. Lucky for me that I am not a black cat for they must hide away at Samain or they may be caught and killed, or even tortured and burnt. Even mildly coloured cats like me are in danger, but for the black ones, it is certain death. It is a harsh time. Some spirits welcome me, some even are glad to see me and might talk to me. Their idle talk is how I know that release from this place is the wish of each one of them; to go on, even if they don't know where or how. They can do nothing here but wait and not know why they wait, but worry they do as they recall to their heart's core ancient sins and accidental wrongs. They hope that this Samain will bring release so that soon they may continue their journey, for good or for ill.

Now here comes the constable. Dundee is his name and he is not a bad sort. As he does each night on his rounds, he glances up at the watchtower, hears the moaning of the wind through the trees and shivers, and although he whistles as he passes and runs his baton along the railings so that it sounds like someone is quickly beating a drum, he still kens that he is passing by a deep place. He is a brave one, Dundee, but this is the least favourite part of his beat.

Spirits crowd up against the fence, leering at him.

'Hey Dundee, look at me!'

'Hey jelly, jiggle some more,' a spirit leans forward with a shriek. 'We don't want your rat-a-tat here.'

I think they are a wee bit cruel. The Constable feels the fright in the air. To be sure, he is a deeply religious man and has no doubt that ghosts are part of God's plan, a part he does nay understand but accepts nonetheless. Grim forebodings come to him each time he passes by this place. Although he sees naught of them, he knows that ghosts are a mix of good and evil, just as they must have been in life; he is afraid and hurries along as fast as he dares. The wind howls around him, lifting his hair. Each night that he goes down to Calton, Dundee meets his soul.

'Hey you, there is something rotten in the state of Edinburgh. Look to it, you loon!' The spirits caper madly, leaping and doffing pretend hats at the constable in his fine uniform. They feed off his fear. This is grand nightly sport for them and they spend their time in thinking up new insults. If they can get Dundee to flinch even a wee bit, as he does now, they rejoice with more yells. I jump down to yowl at them all, go over to Dundee in a friendly fashion and walk along with him.

'Ah, Belle,' he says. "Tis time for home and bed, and the same for you, I think.'

25 October

Isla's narrative

I shall have some fun with them today. Och! What will I nay get up to, now no one can see me at all? I am on the lookout for someone particular, someone I want to put paid to, who tried to steal my man, aye. She will be sorry before the day is over.

The shop is busy this morning, aye, a wee bit too busy I ken. I watch the door, looking out for Duncan, counting people as they come and go. What a fine laugh

I have. Lots of them hardly ever step foot in here. I hear their whispers; they are here for a good gossip and to find out how I died.

Mrs. McIver wants her potion. Mr. Muir tells her she does nay need it yet, but she keeps at him. 'And how is poor Miss Charlotte, Mr. Muir?' Och, butter wouldn't melt but we all know she is an unkind old bat, made up of sour grapes and bitter gall.

'She is distressed, of course, but she seems well enough.' Mr. Muir is standoffish, but Mrs. McIver does nay notice. She kin nay notice a deal of things, Mrs. McIver; I have seen it in her before.

'Aye, I'm glad of it. Some lassies would take such a thing too much to heart.' Her eyes grow brighter. 'And when is the funeral to be?'

'On the Sunday, Mrs. McIver. Here is your mixture. That will be on account?' he asks.

'Thank you, Mr. Muir. And will Mr. Harker be there? I'm sure he's been here quite a bit lately, to care for Miss Charlotte, aye? And a fine young man he seems too, always working so hard at the solicitors, is he not?'

The laughter flies out of me, I canna help it. She is good; I have to hand it to her; she'll be getting blood from a stone soon.

'I'm sure I don't know,' Mr. Muir says carefully. He is holding his own but it is not easy for him, poor man; it has been a long morning and now this nosey hen.

'Aye, it's true. I have seen him with my own eyes. Please pass on my condolences,' says Mrs. McIver. Her eyes change from merely bright to glittering. 'If you

could just tell me when Miss Charlotte will be receiving?'

'I'm sorry, I don't know. If you'll just excuse me, Mrs. McIver! Now, who was next?'

She has to admit defeat at last. Now is my chance to pay her out and for the sheer devilry of it I whisper in her ear, 'Watch out, just you watch out you fine Mrs. McIver!' For a moment her step falters and she puts out her hand to steady herself against the wall, but whether from my words, or because Belle has darted in front of her, I canna tell. It is grand though, to see her so disconcerted.

Seeing the fun is over for the moment, I waft my way up the stairs and into my bedroom where Hannah and Charlotte are sitting. 'Hello, my beauties,' I cry out cheerfully. I see no reason not to, though of course I dinna expect them to reply. Maybe, they will feel my presence and my contentment. Actually, I could quite enjoy myself, if only they didn't look so sad, starin' at my old body resting on the bed; I feel no connection to it, no longing to be back within that skin. I, or rather that lump on the bed, has been newly washed and dressed in my best green velvet gown and slippers. They will be all right to be buried in, I suppose. An ancient slip of the heather, a birthday present from Duncan long ago, is pinned to the bodice. That is nice.

'Have we done everything, do you think, Hannah?' Charlotte points at the candles that stand by the bed head. 'Should these be lit?' Her voice flutters weakly up

from somewhere deep in her breast, reluctant to come out.

'Nay, nay, not till night time . . . now, come along downstairs and wait with me in the kitchen. McArthur will be here soon to measure for the coffin.' Hannah is brisk and businesslike; she is right to be so, for it's what the lassie needs.

I go along with them, glad to see that they are doing their best. I feel proud of them, the strength they show, and verra fond. I would like to let them know I am alright, that I am fine an' there is nothing at all for them to worry about. It's a useless wish, I ken, but I canna help it.

Hannah brings Charlotte sharply past the shop, not pausing to greet anyone from the town, and they disappear into the kitchen. There must be a real chill in the air, for the two of them move straight to the fire where my fine lady Belle has come and is stretched out on the hearth. Charlotte stoops to pick her up, and holding her close to her breast, strokes and pets her, while all the while Belle, resting in her arms, keeps her eyes on me.

'What shall we do?' Charlotte asks.

She sounds so low, so lost, not at all like herself, that my heart breaks and Hannah stares at her in dismay. She's a right bonnie lassie, with her fine dark hair bound up around her head, but her eyes are hollow, her mouth turns down, and she fidgets in front of the fire. Poor wee thing, that's the last of her kin gone, and her only seventeen.

'Well, my chick, we'd best get started with the bak-

ing,' Hannah says briskly. 'Only three days to the funeral and lots to be done.'

I nod, not that anyone can see. That's right! Keep her busy!

Pulling out a long metal tray, Hannah begins to rummage in the pantry, letting loose a wee cloud of flour. She hums and looks around, pretends to want for this and that. At length Charlotte lets Belle down and begins tying on her apron so that Hannah begins to chat of what to bake, and to put cheer into her voice.

I drift back up the staircase; in truth it is too sad for me in that kitchen. My mood has changed; there's no fun in being dead there now, none at all. The bedroom has gone dark, although the window lets in a wee bit of light so I go over to have another look at myself. I'm dressed up like a queen in my beautiful green velvet, and if I still had a bit of the auburn in my hair I might look all right. But seeing myself on that bed, I ken for the first time now just how old I looked to others. I thought I knew, aye. I'd look in the mirror and preen. But no, now I see that I dinna look like I ken I did at all, not with that wrinkly neck and sorry complexion! And my fingers are long and bony now that I see them without any work in hand, no knitting needles or crochet hooks, nor any Good Book to read. Well, what do I care? Now I'm as light as air. I glide out of the room as easily as I entered it, down the stairs and into the kitchen once more where I watch with a sad sort of contentment. I would like to join in, tell them to use the older eggs, not the ones newly laid, and not to use so much dripping in the pastry, but what a hope!

Belle, circling around my feet, eyes me cautiously; aye, Belle is aware of me, that is for certain. She knows. Still keeping an eye on me, she keeps glancing over to the busy fingers that work with forbidden food, ready to pounce on any morsel that drops from the bench. 'Ye understand me, don't ye, Belle? It is not just the waste that I am worried over; it is how the cakes and tarts will turn out. Och! I suppose they've been working their own way, ever since I took to my bed.' I begin to laugh as I think of the ridiculous predicament I am in, seething with frustration in my own kitchen, worried about my own funeral!

The cooks concentrate on their tasks, grateful, I suppose, that some things still have to be done, things that take no notice of death. Charlotte checks the kettle on the hob before bending down in front of the oven. Just as I taught her, she opens the oven door and waves her hand inside to gauge the temperature. Not quite hot enough yet for baking. Stooping lower, she opens the door beneath where the fire burns and adds a few pieces of wood. Hannah watches her from the corner of her eye; like me, she seems glad to see her occupied. Och, I ken grief well enough, that overwhelming wave of sadness and fatigue, for have I not grieved for my Dunc these many years? I ken my chicks are sad and serious, sending up silent prayers and fighting their desire to cry or to rest. But I hope to help and try to send a feeling of

comfort to their hearts. The three of us have had many
a fine time and some hearty laughs in this kitchen.

Belle's narrative

I doze in the sun; it is my favourite thing to do and
the windowsill of the shop is a perfect spot for me.
Not that there be a lot of sunshine at the minute.
But I am comfortable until the wee Scottie that lives
in the street takes up his infernal barking and wakes
me. I shall give him a lesson one of these days. After
I feed up on scraps and bits of cockroaches, I head
out to have a look round the town, beginning with
the Thistle. The first sight I spy is Tom and Crowe in
their usual nook, doing nothing much, just drinking
and staring out the window and sometimes having a
game of dominoes. Tom is sliding his empty beaker
back and forth between his two rough hands, getting
faster and faster, and more and more reckless until it
begins to rock. 'Look, Crowe!' I huddle near them to
hear what they are saying, and maybe Tom, who is a
big softie, will give me a bite to eat.

'Settle down, Tom! The day be long, and you won't
hurry it along with fretting. Bide a while, man, use yer
noggin! Do ye think we have so many places to go?'

Tom grins and looks sheepish. He puts down his
beaker and glances around, drumming his awkward
fingers on the table.

'Have ye an appointment at the castle, then? Is the
Lord Chamberlain expectin' ye?' Crowe asks.

'No, no.' Tom begins to hum. 'Can we play dominoes, Crowe?'

Crowe shrugs.

Tom gets the board and begins to set up the game. 'Can I have another bun, Crowe?'

'Not yet, Tom! Let's have the game first.' Crowe moves a domino into position.

'This is my favourite,' Tom says, indicating the domino he now places. 'See how it has this mark on it, it looks just like a wee doggie.' And indeed it does, drat the animals.

Crowe glances around the room, seeing a few other idlers, men he knows have no work, or thieves like him. He raises his glass and puts it down again without drinking; he has to make it last.

'C'mon, Crowe! Ye haven't moved yet.'

Midnight and I am again at Dr. Walters chambers, not inside but staring through his window at the fire. I'm grateful for my nice fur coat, but still I would rather be inside than out here in the cold night air. The doctor sits at his scarred desk, his back to the fire, and the whiskey bottle dozing in the corner. A large medical tome lies open before him. His eyes race over the diagrams on the well-thumbed pages. He writes in a small notebook and turns the pages of the volume until he comes to a chapter that displays sections of the larynx, trachea and diaphragm. He can get no more clues from them. I expect he has examined and puzzled over them a dozen times before. Locating his case notes for Flora Ferguson, he spreads his large fingers over the word 'consumption' as if he can destroy the disease by blotting it out. I watch and sympathize. His gaze travels from his notes to the diagrams and back again and his shoulders sag. Rising, the doctor goes to the table and rests his hands on it, taking the weight on his wrists, and stares straight ahead, watching the trees bending in the wind. After a time, he looks around the room, his eyes pass over me as if I was not there. Indeed, likely he cannot see me in the dark outside the glass. Nay, it is the whiskey bottle beckons him. His lips firm into a straight line and he looks heavenward. The bottle does a wee jig in the firelight, cooing like a dove and smiling invitingly. Dr. Walters turns back to his desk, gazes for a moment into the splutter of the candle. In a moment, he knows, it will die, just as patients do. Opening a drawer, he pulls out another candle, lights it and pushes it down into the hot wax until it is fixed in place. I know his thoughts well enough and sad thoughts they are.

He feels for them all, all those he canna help. But it is Flora that has stirred him. Flora. Something must be done, and he is desperate enough to do it, but does not know at all what will save her. I feel sad, too — I have caught it from him. I turn and head for home and the window that is left open a crack, just enough for me to slip under. How kind they are! In I go and settle down once more on my Isla's bed, so comfy but with no warm body to snuggle up to now. She is not so far away. I know it and I feel her past kindnesses around me.

26 October

Belle's narrative

'Well, it won't be long now.' In the outer office good-looking Luke Harker is beaming.

'No, it was looking a little close there for a while,' Charels nods.

Back at the solicitor's office, I am afraid there may be squalls ahead. And right I am, for here comes the old man, moving slowly out of his room and over to the fire where he stoops to warm his hands. McCormack's bent figure invites pity as he moves forward, leaning heavily on his cane. He frowns, though it is difficult to see through the long white beard that, except for the yellow brown nicotine stains that stipple it, matches the thinning hair on his head. 'What are ye doing blithering here, Luke? Have ye no work to do?' A cross voice. Luke immediately returns to his desk and begins to write, head down to hide the scowl on his face.

'Mr. Charels,' McCormack continues in a grim tone. 'I'd like a word with ye.'

Uh-oh. That villain Charels is about to get his

come-uppance for good and all. None of us have liked the man since he came here.

'Let's not beat around the bush, Charels, a verra grave situation has arisen. There's a lot of money gone missing.'

Charels looks blank, shocked. He takes a moment before answering and his tone is as forceful and convincing as he can make it. 'It can't be . . . it simply cannot be. I check every cent that goes through this office. And Luke Harker records and banks it. He is meticulous! It has to be an accounting mistake, perhaps at the bank.'

'The bank!' McCormack thunders. 'I've just been to the bank and could nay even draw out ten pound. The account has been nearly emptied! And by whom? People, companies, trusts I have never even heard of.' He fixes his partner with a glare; his angry face and accusing eye, despite his old age and stooped figure, glue Charels to the spot.

Luke hears his raised voice, winces at the occasional word, and seems to know very well what it is about. He keeps his head down while he thinks furiously; he appears to be in a state of barely controlled, quiet panic, although the others, caught up in their argument, do not notice.

'Two weeks past I was paid for acting as executor for the McGillivray's. There was a fair bit of money involved. I paid thirty pound into the general account, where it should still be, sir! And is not!'

Charels moves his staring eyes downward to encompass his feet and I make sure I am far away from them.

'Well, sir! What have you to say?' McCormack thunders at him.

'I'm sure there's a reasonable explanation, Mr. Mc-Cormack. We do have bills, rent and coal and wages and so forth. I'll be checking on it right away.'

'See to it, man! I know when something's not as it should be.' McCormack raises his finger and points it shakily at Charels. 'We might be partners, but I won't be diddled by you.' Much older than the middle-aged Charels, he begins to cough. Slowly lowering himself, McCormack sits down, bringing out his handkerchief and covering his face, which has become as red as the fire burning in the grate.

Becoming solicitous Charels brings him a cup of water. 'I'll get to the bottom of it,' he says, 'it'll be my priority from now on.'

What a load of old cobblers is what I say! And I'll wager McCormack says it too.

Charels hurries from the main office, the hardness of his averted eyes telling Luke to keep working quietly and ask no questions until they can meet elsewhere. Back in his own room, Charels, truly shaking now, sits down and places his head in his hands. He groans softly. He opens a drawer, pulls out some papers and stares at them, blank eyed. He scribbles down some figures, making a poor pretence of working. Opening and shutting drawers, pushing his paperweight back and forth. He doesn't fool me!

In the outer office Luke's scowl slowly disappears; obviously, he decides, he is not suspected. It is only Charels at this stage. But it may spread to him. Well, if it comes to that, he will be ready. He is a soft man; he does not like violence. But he knows those who do and he will employ them if need be. Quietly, he returns to his ledgers. I leave these villains and go with old man McCormack back into his own office. I sit up on his desk and commiserate with him. He pats me kindly, cooing and searching my eyes. 'It's a fine mess,' he snorts, 'a fine mess, my Belle. He'll make it his priority, my arse!'

Isla's narrative

It is fine and dry, early evening and all goes on around me; I join in of course, but no one hears me, which brings a feeling of mischievous merriment! I can be as rude as I like. This Luke now, he is an interesting one for sure. I find that Hannah likes him no more than I, but I'll wager she cannot put a finger on what it is, not any more than I can. I just feel it, and it's so strong, the atmosphere around him; it is not only him, but the space he moves in, that is amiss. Quite wrong. I look and look but only become more puzzled. He is certainly verra polite and respectable. Charlotte seems to adore him. If only Duncan were here! He would know what is awry with the man.

Luke and Charlotte sit together on the couch while Hannah is in the nearby chair, all neatly grouped around the fire. The remains of tea and cake are on the table; Charlotte and Hannah have been baking all day for the funeral and they are taking a wee sample.

'There will be a lot of people,' Hannah says. 'All those who've come to the shop over the years, as well as friends.'

'Will young Kenny come and play the fiddle for us, do you think, Hannah?' asks Charlotte in a fretful tone. Her voice still catches as she speaks.

Luke leans forward. 'I will see to it,' he says. 'Don't worry. I'll talk to him tomorrow in the office.' He strokes her hand with his own which is soft and flabby, like a baby's. He is a slimy wee mannie; not that it isn't fine for a man to stroke your hand — nay, it can be grand. But this Luke Harker: - he is as slimy as a toad, I'll warrant.

'I'm glad it's to be tomorrow. If God is kind, it will not rain.' Charlotte wraps her arms around herself and pulls her shawl tighter.

'Are you cold, my love?' asks Luke.

'Nay, it is nay cold that affects me,' she shakes her head.

As they sit quietly for a while, I continue to examine Luke carefully. He is very good-looking and I can forgive the lassie for finding him attractive. I may have fallen for him myself at Charlotte's age. He speaks well; his manners are polished. But to be sure the man does not have a joke in him, nothing that might lift her mood, and what good is a lad without that?

The clock strikes the hour. Rising briskly, Hannah

begins to clear away the tea things. 'It's past nine o'clock, Mr. Luke,' she says. 'Tomorrow will be drear enough; it's time we were all abed.'

Luke rises obediently and turns to Charlotte, kisses her hand. He gives Hannah a blank look, but I feel an angry current coming from him that lashes me like a strong wind. 'I will be here first thing. Don't worry,' he repeats. 'I'll be with you all day.' He goes to the door and looks back at Charlotte as he puts on his hat and coat, but she does not look up, merely holds herself tighter as she stares at the fire. Hannah shuts the door behind him, giving it a wee kick as she shoots the bolt. Ha ha! no pulling the wool over her eyes!

'We would normally be upstairs now, saying good-night to Grandma,' Charlotte whispers; again, I feel a deep sadness for her, left so young with no family to care for her. I move close, trying to comfort the lass and who knows if it does any good? Hannah picks up the candle and brings Charlotte gently to her feet; she leads her along, up the old wooden staircase and into her room. Using her candle, Hannah lights the one at the bedside and bids her goodnight with a hug.

'It will be all right,' Hannah says. 'It may be difficult tomorrow but I believe we will get through it weel enough.'

'Aye. Good night, Hannah.'

'Sleep well, my chick.'

After Hannah leaves, Charlotte looks around, as if confused, as if she has landed in a place she has never seen before. She does everything slowly, removing her *clothes, pulling her white muslin nightgown down over her head, and hanging up her dark day dress and speckless white apron. She kneels next to her bed and folds her hands; her lips move and a tear falls. I stay at her side as she climbs like a sleepwalker into bed. Her face is so white and weary as she pulls the covers up and rolls over to stare out the window that I am undone. Aye, it is perfect for the night before a funeral, cold and dark while restless branches wave against the blue black of the sky. We are all so empty, and for my Charlotte I am sadder than I kin say.*

Tomorrow that old body, so useless to me now, will be buried.

Tomorrow I will make some changes.

27 October

Belle's narrative

It is time to leave for the funeral; already Luke and Charels are late when there is a knock at the door.

I have been out early to Calton Burial Ground to see how the land lay and now I am back again and on watch. Some people have already gathered in the street outside the apothecary shop, but here at the solicitor's they are still blithering. And I am sure Miss Charlotte will not begin without her precious Luke.

'Mr. Charels?' asks the messenger on the doorstep. 'Two letters for you, sir.' Instinctively Charels knows that this is what they have been expecting for weeks, have been on tenterhooks for. Trying to hide his feelings, a strange mixture of anxiety and delight, Charels gives him a penny and takes the letters inside, scrutinizing the envelopes for any clue to the tone of their news.

Luke and Charels seem much more anxious to read their correspondence than to go to the funeral. That can wait for here is important news, the most important they can imagine. They examine the two envelopes, both stamped with some indecipherable black ink, no return address, but with different handwriting on each. Luke grabs them both and opens one. They read it greedily, before turning to look at each other with wary eyes.

'Well,' Charels says, 'it is all in hand, if we hold our nerve. Let us do our part.'

'There's naught else we can do,' says Luke, passing the letter back to Charels; the second letter, in a woman's hand, he folds and puts in his pocket without reading it. 'We only need to keep the old bugger off our backs for a little while longer. The funeral should keep him well occupied for today at least.' He glances at the carriage clock on the mantelpiece. 'Time we were going.'

Isla's narrative

Listen now! It is the day of my funeral and I expect to have a most interesting time of it. I am ready for the good things they will say, as well as for the gossip, which will be harsh I do not doubt. And if I do not find my Duncan today I will be verra surprised. The burial ground is the place for us ghosts, is it not? And won't I be buried at Calton Burial Ground, right beside him? I am ready.

The procession begins outside the shop; first come two black horses pulling the coffin on a long dray, then Charlotte and Luke Harker, with everyone else slowly shuffling behind. They move slowly along Princes Street and down Waterloo, leaving behind the Old Town with its ragged but solid feel. I have a fine black coffin with gleaming brass handles; the horses are done up a treat with their manes in glossy braids and I feel . . . I feel, not the lump in my throat that I expected, but devilment rising in me again. Their grim faces with their eyes straight ahead need a wee bit of gingering up, is what it is. I never liked the long faces. I should like to make them all laugh, just a wee bit, even if it is a funeral.

Hannah, her black clothes not becoming her as they do Charlotte, stays close to her mistress, who looks as pale and beautiful as a faery. The old people Dunc and I have known for decades do not seem too dour. I got quite used to going to funerals myself, before I took to my bed. I paid my respects to the dead as was right and proper, but after, with a drink in my hand, well, it was grand to see old friends and hear their news. And now I am right glad to see them walking along, though it makes me sad to see that they struggle a wee bit with the climb. There is no rain, but the sky threatens, dark and cloudy. Here and there someone pulls out a flask and passes it around. Belle stalks the horses' hooves and misses being kicked by a hairsbreadth, so that it makes me laugh to watch her.

I glide along, looking at all the folk, staring into their faces, and occasionally talking to Charlotte or Hannah. 'Buck up,' I say. 'If this is death, it's not all that dreadful. And don't I wish you could hear me!'

Charlotte's eyes are blank under her black mourning bonnet. Her hand rests on Luke's arm but it keeps slipping off and each time he brings it up again. After a time he puts his arm around her, looking more at her than at anything else. Charlotte does not take her eyes off the coffin, no, not to look at the bouncing legs of the horses clop clopping along the road, or at the nearly leafless trees bending against the shifting, louring sky. She looks at the black wood that holds that old body of mine, but I'll swear she does not see the coffin at all; nor do I. No, I am alive and laughing as I bring the bread out of the oven and Charlotte's 10-year-old self comes running into the kitchen to ask for a slice.

'The Lord is my shepherd, I shall not want . . . ' The crowd recites the psalm with Pastor Furphy. Och, they are all cold and longing for a nip. A fine mist glistens on the bonnets of the ladies and hats of the men; I ken well how the cold wetness seeps onto the backs of their ears and into the fine crevices of their skins so that even a light wind makes them shiver; and here am I not feeling it at all. I smile at Belle in her fur coat. In a way it is grand.

Pastor Furphy comes up to Charlotte and looks at her kindly, saying, 'My dear, this is not the time or place for a eulogy. Let us save that for later when we are all snug around the fire. That is what Isla would have wanted, I'm sure.' I nod like a puppet; it is best to get the child and all of them out of the bitter cold. 'You need not worry; I will speak and you will not have to say a word if you do not wish.'

Charlotte takes his hand in hers and nods. The coffin is gently lowered into the ground next to my Dunc. She casts her dried heather onto it. Hannah follows. Their tears fall now, now that the earth is falling onto the wooden lid with soft shuddering plops. 'Good bye Grandma', Charlotte whispers.

I nearly cry myself, but rather than that I call out, 'I'm not going anywhere, not till I'm with my Duncan again!' The words are shouted without me thinking much; with all that's been happening I have almost forgotten to look for him, but he is always there, in the back of my mind. And now, surely, it is time for him to appear. So where is he?

Hannah moves forward to stand on Charlotte's side, holding her arm that looks so fragile and thin compared to Hannah's thick and sturdy one. Planting her feet firmly on the ground, Hannah looks as strong and solid as a rock as the folk passing by stop to shake her hand or embrace her, as well as Charlotte. 'She was a good woman,' they say, or 'I will miss her.' They only make *them greet more, poor hens and the warm tears moisten their cheeks. Mrs. McIver for once stays silent as she gives Charlotte a long embrace. The trio of Luke Harker, Charlotte and Hannah stand together, their expressions fixed, their bodies still, their words very low. The old Randall sisters, still dressing alike after all these years, with long grey hair pinned up and matching burgundy cloaks and hats, approach and say, 'We knew her all our lives. She was a grand friend.' Aye, it's nice to hear. They have outlived me, and them older than me by six years. Charlotte thanks them all shakily and invites them back for a wee bite. Only when the last person has spoken to them, does the trio turn and begin the long walk back. They move slowly, stiffly, for home. And me, a mere piece of mist in the moist air, I move with them. I am beyond disappointed in not finding my Duncan, beyond wondering what can be wrong that he does not come. In fact, I am beginning to be angry.*

Belle's narrative

Before the funeral, I remained for a while with old McCormack, as kind a man who ever lived; he gave me a saucer of milk and stroked my back. I grieve for him. Those two villains are taking advantage of him somehow and neither he nor I know how to stop them.

Mr. McCormack did not go to the funeral; someone should always be in the office is the tale he told to his friends, but really he had his own small project to see through while Luke and Charels were away. Of course, he still meant to attend the wake, but first he had to act upon his suspicions and find out the truth.

An iron ring laden with heavy keys appeared out of Mr. McCormack's deep pocket. He held it up and rattled it, looking and feeling with his fingers for the keys to the desks that he wished to investigate. Going into Charels' office, he unlocked his drawer, pulled out his papers and carefully examined them, keeping them in order. He grunted. After a time, he collapsed back into the chair and grunted again.

'What is going on, my fine wee Belle?' Mr. McCormack asked me. 'Where is the money going?' I wished I could answer him. 'It is all so tidily done,' he added after a long pause. With an effort, he lifted himself from the chair. After replacing all the papers exactly as they were and relocking the drawer, he left the office to look at Luke's desk; the tidiness there made him despair of finding anything. Again he inserted a key into the desk drawer, from which he extracted more and different documents. He examined them closely. It took him a while, but at the end he sighed and lifted his bleary eyes to stare out the window.

After making a few notes, McCormack tucked them into his pocket, replaced the papers and relocked the desk. He moved heavily back to his own office and quickly wrote a letter, settled back into his chair. Soon his mouth fell open, as he fell fast asleep with his head tilted back on the headrest. Time to go! I slipped out through the window and raced down to join the procession and the funeral.

Isla's narrative

I stand beside Mr. Muir as he waits, ready to open the heavy wooden door to the street; it swings back on its hinges with a creak every time a body enters. As he welcomes each of them his solemn face changes to a smile. I half want to be there in the flesh, and half feel glad to be invisible. I watch and listen, and I do something else. I feel an odd sensation of being aware of their temper; of feeling quite exactly as this or that person is feeling. As each one comes near to me, I pick up their mood and something of their thoughts. You may say the living do this as well and you are right. I did it myself. But this is so much stronger, so much clearer and more knowing, that I am fascinated.

Hannah, Charlotte and Mr. Muir too, I am sure, have worked hard to make people welcome. I am pleased with their preparations; of course the shop is closed to business in honour of the funeral. It becomes more and more crowded as the mourners return from Calton Burial Ground. The room is decorated with dry flowers and they have rearranged the furniture to fit in more people; a good fire crackles in the grate. With plates of small cakes and glasses of port ready poured on the dining table, everything has been done to make people feel comfortable. It's almost like I'm a lass again, welcoming everyone to my wedding breakfast, except that everyone is so sombre.

'Isla and I were from the same wee village and just the same age, you know,' says a small woman to Mr.

Muir. I stare; I don't remember the voice, but I do remember her face and her as a laughing lassie always likin' to put the heather in her hair. I suppose she could be as old as me. She smiles as if triumphant at having outlived me. 'Isla was always a definite one, certain of what she wanted.' Aye, I was always that, to be sure.

Small groups dot the room, sitting or standing. Kenny Silver props his violin case carefully in the corner. Aye, the whole lot is nice and comfortable. When Mr. Muir opens the door to admit Charlotte, Luke and Hannah everyone moves forward a step, then stops uncertainly. Charlotte looks around, her eyes teary.

I feel for her, dragged down to see the state she is in. 'I'm fine,' I want to exclaim. 'Look, here I am.' But that is foolish.

Here, let me tell you how it goes. Luke clears his throat and opens his mouth to speak, but Hannah quickly ushers Charlotte forward. Luke is a bit stunned at this and shoots a dark look at Hannah. Ha ha! Everyone looks quietly at Charlotte, who loses her bewildered air as she looks around at their friendly encouraging faces.

'Thank ye all for coming,' her voice is a wee bit low and shakes some but she goes on. 'Ye are all welcome to stay and celebrate Isla's life. There is plenty of food and drink for all.' By the end she sounds almost strong.

Mrs. McIver comes forward immediately, shaking Charlotte's hand and embracing her.

'I know you must be feeling very gloomy, my dear, but you can come to me anytime. I'd love to have ye.'

She smiles and her words are kind, but her eyes bore into Charlotte's soul, the horrible old bat! When Charlotte allows the teardrops to spill down her cheeks, Mrs. McIver leads her to a chair; and Hannah urges a bumper of brandy into Charlotte's hand.

Like an obedient child, Charlotte drinks the brandy and wipes her face with her hands, and then with a tiny lace handkerchief. 'It's kind of you, Mrs. McIver. Thank you, I will see.' Luke hovers above Charlotte every bit as useless as a shag on a rock.

I'm glad to see that even if Luke does not know what to do, John Muir does. He goes around the room chatting and refilling glasses and signals to Kenny Silver to start playing. Some good Scottish airs will cheer up my chick. Picking up his violin and drawing the bow across the strings, Kenny begins a slow lilting song of Robbie Burns. It is neither happy nor sad music, but simply present with the ebb and flow of melody and rhythm. Kenny is good, plays well enough to help people relax a bit and begin to talk. Some tap their feet. Happy to be away from the chilly entry, Mr. Muir stations himself close to the fire. A good host, scoops up a glass of punch and places it near Kenny's elbow.

The Reverend positions himself by Charlotte's chair so that when Mrs. McIver rises, he takes her place. He begins to talk easily of nothing much; the weather, his horse, the next sermon he is planning. Charlotte summons a smile for him but canna keep it in place. Luke stays as close as he can to her, not speaking to anyone. I can tell he does not feel any comfort here. He looks around for a chair but the old people have taken them all. Placing his hand on Charlotte's shoulder, he murmurs in her ear, 'I'm just behind you, my love.' He should have been on the stage; he is a braw play actor, for again I feel that although his words are fine, his feeling is all wrong. The man sickens me. Kenny plays his fiddle louder now, loosing wild highland airs into the room, each one following on the heels of the last. Hannah comes in laden with bread, cheese and butter, followed by Mr. Muir who carries steaming roast mutton and potatoes. Guests crowd around the table, helping themselves, delighted to have the gift of food to save them from speaking words when they do not know what to say. The young people, Charlotte's friends, seem tentative, still a wee bit afraid of funerals.

The fire burns high, sending sparks racing up the chimney. They remind me to rub my wedding ring, but the sparks that rise still bring no Duncan. Hmm! The fire and the many folk present must be warming the room, for people are removing their shawls and coats and hats. Hannah comes and goes to the kitchen, bringing in haggis followed by grand wee tarts and oatcakes.

I roam around, listening to different conversations, losing myself in their talk. What a long time it's been since I've been in a crowd!

'Belle!' Hannah calls sharply. 'Get away from the table — off ye go!' She shoos the cat out the door. Out I float with her and together we look back at the scene through the small square panes of the window. All my old friends are inside, talking, some laughing now, some

letting loose a tear. It's nice to see them all together, all enjoying themselves. The drinks go round again. It's a good funeral.

Belle circles my feet.

'It's not for us, eh my Belle?'

'Yeow.' At that, my splendid tabby leaps like a champion up onto the windowsill and settles her body comfortably along its ledge. Her eyes blaze. She sees me all right, and hears me too. It is a blessing that at least one of God's creatures knows I'm here.

'I shall go back in a wee bit though,' I whisper to Belle. 'I must. I canna miss my own wake, now, can I? I'm out here just for the perspective, ye ken. It is all a bit close for me, and no one to talk to. Ye'll just have to do.' Belle gives a large yawn and begins to lick her fur with her raspy tongue, grooming and stretching. 'Sure, I wish I was a cat like ye, and had no worries at all but where the next wee mouse is coming from.' I gaze beyond her, my Belle, back through the window at all the busyness. 'Yon Kenny plays grandly, does he not? Well, off I go.' Gently I manoeuvre my way back into the room and fetch up near the fire, watching the burning embers drop under the grate as above them the flames rise red and bright. Aye, it is a very good funeral, yet I am feeling dull, for it is obvious that Duncan is not coming.

Belle's narrative

Seeing as the wake nearly over, I've taken myself off to the Thistle. Already far gone in drink, Sandy frightens me and I stay by the fire; but I can still hear every word, and so can everyone here. We all know that something that we don't really want to know about is going on.

'Ah, ye were an innocent babe when ye first came to me,' chuckles Sandy.

Crowe gives him the death stare but Sandy is has had too many whiskeys to care.

'Aye, an innocent babby, fresh from the orphanage, still blithering about right and wrong, God and the devil. Dinna have a clue how to look after yerself.' Sandy throws back his head and laughs, his green satyr's eyes narrowing and his red hair hanging loose and floating like the devil's helpmeet.

'Leave it Sandy. We've all heard the tale often enough,' says Crowe. He nods to Tom to continue with their game of dominoes. 'Why do ye come to plague us now?'

Sandy laughs harder, placing his hand on his ribs and gasping for breath. 'Tom, such a snivelling bairn he was, ye'd . . . '

'On yer feet!' Crowe jumps up, sending the pieces flying. 'Enough!'

'Aye, and ye always were a short-tempered bastard of a man.' Sandy wipes his eyes. 'Sit down, sit down, we're all friends here.' He signals to the man at the bar, who has stopped his work to stare — a big man, always happy to chuck someone out. 'Bring us more ale.'

'Yer no friend of mine, Sandy, and well do ye know

it.' Crowe's black eyes move from Sandy to the window where the frost on the tree branches glistens; he'd like to leave, if it was not so cold outdoors.

Tom has shrunk bank in his seat. He eyes both men guardedly.

'Yer mighty unfriendly, Crowe, mighty unfriendly, when I am here to bring ye work.'

'We're not interested,' Crowe snaps. Slowly he lowers himself back into his seat. 'Pick up the pieces Tom,' he orders brusquely and Tom stoops to obey; he does not like the arguing.

A fresh pitcher arrives on the table, and Sandy tops up the three beakers. 'There's another body wanted.' Now he keeps his voice low.. 'Sometime next week. Ye'd like that, wouldn't ye, Tommy lad?'

'Keep your voice down, ye fool! Anyway, we have our own arrangements,' says Crowe. 'We don't need yours.'

Down on the floor Tom concentrates on searching for dominoes. He is too frightened to give Sandy any sort of answer, and besides he would only stammer and not know what to say.

'It's a new man wants it.' Sandy has lowered his voice to a mere whisper, but Crowe only glares at him.

Tom sits back up on the bench, the dominoes in his hands. A wee bit white around the gills, he resets the board, looking to Crowe for approval.

'And if ye're smart ye'll stay away from Walters for a while,' adds Sandy. 'He's getting a bit greedy. I give ye the warning for free, though I don't know why, when ye are such a prick.'

I would like to scratch his eyes out!

Crowe sucks on his pipe; he is ready to fight, ready to head out the door and stuff Sandy's head in the dirt. The space of the air between them bristles with a tense electricity.

Tom, having reset the board, waits, staring out the window at a group of pheasants that run about the yard. Their delicate brown, white, red and yellow feathers occasionally ruffle and shine when hit by the rays of the setting sun. He is entranced, as if wanting to go out and touch them, for the sake of the peace of them, away from the tension in here. As the light thickens, they rise to roost among the branches.

For a moment longer Sandy sits, but soon he shoves back his chair and forgoing his usual caution, he leaves the Thistle with a muscular bang of the door. It is safe for me to move closer now, sit with Tom and watch the birds.

Isla's narrative

There they are — Hannah, Charlotte and Luke — eating their dinner verra glumly indeed. Afterwards, with Belle in her lap, Charlotte reads aloud from Matthew as they sit by the fire. She has a fine clear voice, not slipping here and there as mine would do. It is very late and all the mourners have gone. Charlotte huddles in Luke's arms, drawing strength from him, though he does nay have any to give. It is a strange thing how that works. She needs the strength and draws it, all in her dainty imagination, while he is as unaware as a badger. I dinna like the man, nor his preoccupied air. The clock strikes eleven and thank God he is going. 'Goodbye, my darling,' he says. It seems to me that he is relieved to be on his way at last. He has been giving out agitation all evening, so much easier for me to spot that sort of thing now that I am in spirit form. Hannah watches with her sharp eyes so that he does not hold Charlotte too close or kiss her too fervently. Hannah is the best watchdog I could have left behind; not a thing does she miss. They follow Luke to the door, giving him his hat and gloves, his coat and scarf. It takes him a moment to put all these on and all the while Hannah frowns and clucks, but he is fixed on ignoring her; his expression does not change. My granddaughter seems still in shock at all that has happened, confused-looking, like a hen that canna find her eggs. They say goodnight; Belle and I watch them, both of us suspicious and worried. It is as if I am watching a show at the theatre but Charlotte and Hannah, well, I care about them the most in the all the world. My brain hums with frustration; it hurts to be so absent and unable to help, but at last Luke is out the door, while Belle scoots out with him.

Belle's narrative

It is very cold now outside, with a damp feel in the air and Edinburgh being such a granite-built town.

Crowding darkness hurries Luke along, his footsteps clicking on the hard cobblestones of the road. I follow, heavy with suspicion. I do not trust him to go home, but that is what he does. In fact, he removes his key from his pocket long before he reaches his own door. Letting himself in, he takes a shaky breath and quickly lights the only lamp in the room. It blazes up in the blackness before drawing down to a steady flame. Changing out of his grey silk waistcoat and his fine clothes, he takes the letters out of his satchel before getting into bed. After reading them again, he is more than ever nervous, that is plain to see. I ken that he needs to stick to the plan, but feels that everything is so crushed and tight. Still feeling Charlotte in his arms, he knows she has complete trust in him, and when he thrusts down the letters, it is as if disgusted with himself for letting things go so far. For a wild moment he cries out aloud that he must tell her the truth, but no doubt his imagination lets him see how the terrible weight of his confession would be reflected in her face. He cannot do it; let her discover his perfidy when he is not around. Aye, how can ye like the man? His own cowardice he pushes away, down deep in the darkness, but he cannot ignore he sight of his shaking hands. Unnerved, he shoves them under the covers, out of sight. Another dram is what he needs, to steady him; aye, and another. Though the fire spits and snaps comfortably, I'll wager that Luke will lie awake long into the night. But I must away.

We cats have a great reputation for laziness, but the truth is we have to spend so much time waiting that we may as well sleep; we will know instantly and wake if anything happens. Really, I am so rushed off my feet caring for this one and that one, that I don't know how I survive it. And then I have to listen to people chiding me for lying about. If they only knew! Like now, for example, I must contrive to make a noise, or enough disturbance to get Luke to rouse and let me out or I will miss my usual graveyard patrol. And surely I must be there on this night, with so much happening. Like Isla, I wonder what has happened to Duncan.

28 October

Isla's narrative

We are gathered in the kitchen again — me, Charlotte, Hannah and Belle — and I listen to their conversation.

'It will be Samain verra soon. I can hardly believe it has come around again so quick like,' says Hannah. 'Remember last year how it was with all the big fires burning and the weans in their silly masks running through the crowds.' Hannah is rolling out pastry and Charlotte is watching intently. She has not learned the knack of the pastry yet, and Hannah makes the best in the city. 'It is a festival I've always enjoyed, even if it scares me some.'

'I don't think I will go this year, Hannah,' says Charlotte.

Ah, that is disappointing.

'But ye must go. Otherwise it is disrespectful to the dead.'

That's right; ye don't want to risk that!

'I would rather not; I could keep Samain here at home, have a wee fire by myself. It seems wrong to be merry-making so soon after Grandma's death.'

'But now you know, my chick, that your Grandma would want you to go.'

In my corner, I nod. 'Aye that I would.' And I could swear that Belle nods with me.

They are quiet. After a wee while Hannah asks, 'Will Mr. Luke be coming tonight?'

'Aye,' says Charlotte listlessly. 'I think I will walk out to the castle, Hannah, and have a bit of a look at the town. It will freshen me.'

'Shall I come with ye?' asks Hannah.

'No, thank ye all the same. I want to go alone . . . maybe later we can go down to the burial ground together.'

'Good morning, ladies,' says John Muir, coming through the door.

'Good morning,' Hannah and Charlotte chorus.

I feel so comfortable and at home with them all. Everything happens as it has happened every morning that I can recall for a long time, until I was forced to take to my bed. I just wish I could pull Duncan into the kitchen too, out of thin air or otherwise.

'How quiet the shop seems this morning,' Mr. Muir says. He goes to the teapot on the table and pours himself a cup, adds a drop of water from the iron kettle simmering on the hob. Settling down on the long bench he says, 'it's been so quiet today I've not heard a speck of gossip.' He grins. 'Not even Mrs. McIver has been in.'

Hannah laughs. 'There now, that is a thing! And how will ye be keeping Samain, Mr. Muir?'

'I'll be going along with my sister and her bairns. It is a job of work to keep them from running off, despite their fears. It is the eldest sets them on, aye — he's a load a mischief in him.' Mr. Muir throws his head back and laughs out loud. He is a fine-looking man in his way.

That's better; I like to see them having a cheerful conversation.

'It sounds grand, Mr. Muir,' says Charlotte. She shifts her gaze to Hannah who is still rolling out dough at one end of the table. 'I will be going for that walk now, Hannah.' Well, if she must go, she will do so; but I think she should stay and talk, not go mooning off on her own.

Mr. Muir looks after her as she goes out of the kitchen. 'Good bye, Charlotte.'

What is that in his voice? Ah, how much more I ken now that I am in spirit. So it is. And how the poor wee man must be suffering!

Belle's narrative

Charlotte does what she always does when she is

melancholy; she walks. She changes her mind about going to the castle and starts out along the roads to Leith Walk; maybe she just doesn't want to be followed and found. But me, I am following her anyway. Again, as an animal, I do not count, ye see; I am well-nigh invisible. She doesn't often go out in the day, apart from a trip to the shops or to the kirk, where she is safe. But now she is wandering alone, and I am determined to see she comes to no harm, so I follow at her heels, just like a dog. I know she needs time. We walk on, passing the hill and watchtower at Calton Burial Ground without going in; she will be visiting there later with Hannah. Arriving at the Water of Leith Charlotte stands and stares for a long while, her thoughts grim and confused. What should she do? I hope she stays here and does not go back to the kirk, which she sometimes does. It is better here in the open spaces. The light and the freshness of the breeze, the sweetness of the air and the chatter of the birds distract her and make her thoughts move toward them, rather than into herself and her own soul's turmoil. Only the water is a dark and moody blue to match her troubled soul. After a time she begins to lighten a bit, while I observe and count three types of duck; there are a couple of Teal, a white one, and one with soft brown markings, all having a paddle together in the shallows. I am really much more attentive to them than she.

Charlotte is possessed of a speaking countenance; I see the thoughts there as sure as if she were speaking them. What is it like to be a bird with no worries, she wonders, the silly lass. It seems that she wouldn't mind being a duck for a while, right now, now that there is so much uncertainty in her life and her grandmother dead and gone. It would be so calm to glide about on the water with no cares. I could tell her how wrong she is, if I could speak, because those ducks are not calm with me here, but never mind. Neither are they gliding on the pond, no, they have to paddle like mad to move along. There in the distance a gaggle of black swamp hens peck at the ground with bright red beaks. They are always in a flock, and never alone as Charlotte is. I don't think that she wants to be solitary either. No, she would like to be with Luke, to belong to him, to have a secure and recognized place in the world. No, not to feel like she does now, so adrift, so lost without our Isla, and so lonely despite the affection of Hannah. Charlotte is so deeply in love with Luke that she is immersed in it, but how can she know that he really loves her? He insists he does and very strongly does she want to believe. God knows if there was ever a woman who needed a man, she considers it to be herself and now. Nay, lass, ye do not, I want to say, at least not with *that* man. I think that it nags her just a little, somewhere deep down — how does she *know* Luke loves her? How can she be sure? Her expression changes again. Now she is thinking of her parents, if only they had survived. She must put that reflection away and dream of Luke. The day is fine; we look at the ducks.

Her eyes shift to the middle of the water where two glittering white swans glide majestically and she allows the sight too cheer her. Walking along the shoreline, she is delighted when she spots the startling black and white contrast on a pair of Siberian Ibis. Not me, though. They are too big for me to tackle. Still, I crouch on my haunches and watch them intently! They stalk along in step, exactly parallel, before simultaneously turning away from each other and then veering in again, all the while remaining in identical movement, like a couple of dancers, legs linked by stiff cords of invisibility.

Charlotte wonders if perhaps she and Luke will be like that, coming together, moving apart; or perhaps they will stick together as if glued. Or perhaps she just doesn't know anything at all! At least, that's what I think. On the walk back home I take leave of my lass and go on to the Royal Infirmary.

I should mebbe prepare you now, for things are going to get worse for little Flora. You probably have guessed that already, but this time I'm at the hospital, it's fair evening and the sun has set long since. Candles burn in the ward and I sit on Flora's bed, waiting.

'Da!' Flora rises up on her elbow, her face illuminated as Daniel Ferguson comes down the aisle to her bed. She puts Pinkus aside as he bends over to kiss her. He is careful not to disturb the covers, but she throws them back to lean into him and for a few moments his arms enclose her in silence. Both faces content, both pairs of eyes closed, breathing steady. After a time he settles her back on the bed, pulling up the blankets but not letting go of her hand.

'How are you, faither?' Flora asks.

'I am well. Aye, very well, my darlin'. It is you I am wanting to know about.'

Flora can do nothing but beam at him. 'Braw, da, I'm braw as can be.'

Seeing Dr. Walters moving from bed to bed, Daniel settles into his chair to wait. He reaches into his pocket and pulls out a small wooden box that he presses into Flora's hand. I get up to have a look; it is well crafted and polished to a high shine. For me, the thing is how good it smells and I stay close.

'Oh Da, it's beautiful!' Flora examines it carefully from all sides; she grasps it in different ways, trying to open it. Shutting her eyes and running her fingers along its surfaces, she glows with delight. 'How does it open?'

I am wondering the same thing!

'Oh, you must work that out yourself, my darlin'. It is a puzzle box. There is a secret way to open it.'

'Did you make it?'

'Aye.' He nods.

I sense that something strange is happening now, something that is hard to tell; it is as if blanket has fallen over us all. Over Daniel's shoulder a gradual change in the light captures my attention. I tingle from head to foot and stand up and arch my back. Flora's eyes widen as the figure of a woman shadowy and fuzzily defined, emerges from the luminescence. 'Ma?' she asks faintly.

'What?' Daniel stares at his wee daughter, before moving his eyes in the direction of her gaze, but all he sees is the bed opposite, the person in it. Flora's eyes are fixed. She sees her mother; the figure smiles and beckons before it slowly fades. Flora lets out her breath. 'Did you see?' she asks breathlessly. 'Did you . . '

The blanket lifts; sounds of the ward around us come back.

'Hello, Mr. Ferguson,' says Dr. Walters, coming up beside them. 'How are you?'

Well, he does not look too grand, that is for sure and certain. Also for sure and certain is that he would never admit it. 'I'm well, sir. How is my Flora faring?'

'She's doing well, very well, aren't you, Flora?' the doctor says this heartily, as if all the world is grand, the day is grand and all things will be well, very well. We all know this is a lie.

Flora is too dazed from seeing the apparition of her mother to answer so she nods slowly; her eyes, still all lit up and darting about, move up to meet the doctor's. The restlessness of her eyes contrasts with the listlessness of her body, but she stirs herself to sit up tall and pushes down a cough.

The men appear not to notice.

'That's a fine looking box you have there,' the doctor says.

'My Da made it,' she says proudly. 'It's a puzzle

box.' She turns it in her hands, holding it up for him to see. They chat a few moments longer. As Dr. Walters prepares to move on to the next bed, he says, 'I see you have a skill in woodworking, Mr. Ferguson. I'll be in my room in about twenty minutes, if you want to join me. I have a carving you might like to see.' He nods at Flora and departs. Daniel gives a slight start.

'What's the matter, Da?'

'Nothing, my darling.'

Flora knows that he is worried because his face has become stony and set. I wonder if Daniel saw his wife appear out of nothing, or if he saw the change in the light, but I doubt it. Flora holds tight to her puzzle box, holding it up close to her face, turning it slowly this way and that to give it a closer examination. Her small fingers push and pull at the inlaid strips of different types of wood. I love her small fingers, the gentleness of them, their lightness and pale colouring. She turns the beautiful box over and over, searching, but it remains resolutely closed.

Daniel begins to thaw at her persistence; he even smiles. Flora is a good lassie and he seems pleased that he has made something useful to distract her, something small but effective. Soft coughs punctuate Flora's rest as they remain side by side until he must leave. She is careful not to spit out any blood, as she does not want her Da to see; it is pooling in her mouth. On his side, Daniel does not to react to any of the tiny red drops that appear on her lips. 'It is time for me to go, but I'll be back tomorrow,' he tells her. 'Be a good lass for the doctors, won't you? And don't forget your prayers.'

This is my cue to get down and be ready to follow. I want to know what is going to be said in Dr. Walters office, though I can make a good guess.

Flora nods and stretches forward to give him a kiss as he leans over and whispers, 'good night, my darling,' into her ear. She gives him a radiant smile.

Daniel Ferguson moves reluctantly through the corridors of the Royal Infirmary to Dr. Walter's office, knocks at the solid wooden door and listens for the muffled 'come in.' I scoot in with him and hide quietly as the two men face each other, neither speaking nor moving. It is a terrible moment.

'Sit down, Mr. Ferguson,' the doctor says.

'Is she. . . ?' Daniel cannot get the words out. He has ceased to breathe.

'Sit down,' Dr. Walters says again.

Daniel sits, staring attentively at the doctor.

'I'm sorry,' Dr. Walters nods slowly. 'You must prepare yourself. It won't be long.'

All the air in Daniel's body pours out in a rush. He topples forward, just stopping his head from hitting the desk in front of him. He lets out a howl but quickly stifles it, pulling himself up back into his chair and covering his face with his hands. 'No, no,' he cries, moving his hands aimlessly.

The doctor brings him a brandy. 'I'm sorry,' he says. 'She is a grand wee lass.'

Daniel swallows the drink in a gulp, stares at Dr.

Walters, looks away. He takes a moment to compose himself. 'Thank ye for your care of Flora.' He rises to his feet. 'I will go sit with her.' A deep sigh escapes him. 'She will be sleeping now.'

Poor man!

Crowe and Tom, almost blind in the darkness, dig at a newly made grave, two places away from where Isla's gravestone was positioned earlier. I am surprised to see them again so soon. Like Isla, the body was only buried yesterday, poor fold that they are. The grave robbers, absorbed in their work, barely speak. In the deep black of the night, the glimmer of light from the lantern is so faint that it cannot be seen more than ten metres away. Flowing gusts of mist keep them well concealed from the watcher in the tower and they need only be on the lookout for Dundee. Tonight all the birds and animals seem to be present; the owls roosting in the nearby fir trees stare at them with luminous yellow eyes that spook them both, even Crowe. (Not me, I am only waiting for one of them to chance it and I will have her in my jaws. I feel as if I haven't eaten in a week.) A vixen that has delicately picked its way through the maze of graves, shows her pointed black snout then pulls back at the sight of me, while rodents run across the grass, and I am sore tempted to give chase.

'Are you sure about this one?' whispers Tom.

'Of course! Walters told me himself to get this very body – now, tonight. Keep going Tom, we're almost there.'

Tom wants to please, but he feels too frightened to hurry; he is sure now that after his fearful experience of two nights previous, he should have stayed away. He pauses and looks around between each spadeful; in the mist is many a terror. 'There's a ghost!' Shivering horribly, Tom points at nothing. 'Did ye see it, Crowe? Did ye?'

'It's nothing, Tom; 'tis only the wind. It blows the fog about, making shapes, ye ken.'

'It's a spirit, I tell ye! They dinna want us here,' Tom digs jerkily, expecting trouble. He doesn't know what, he just wants to go, get away from the black damnation of Calton and never come back. He hears Crow's voice as he sporadically talks to him, the words indistinct but the tone calm, reassuring, and cheerful, but he is so lost in his fear he can't make out the words.

Tom is right of course; the spirits are there, and they are hopping mad.

'Damn yer black hearts! Digging up these poor old bones, for profit! Why if I had a body still, I'd give ye what for! A body!' shouts the spirit of an old man.

Other spirits crowd around, railing at the diggers. They enjoy the shouting and the turmoil; they have grown used to whoever comes to the burial ground, but reserve their hate for those who dig up bodies. None of them can tolerate that, no matter how they disagree on other things. Soon it will be Samain and they will shout more, much more, they hope, and hope to be seen. They are glad to get a wee bit of practice.

'Get away, ye villains, ye black hearts!'

'Leave us in peace!'

'Do ye want a haunting, me fine ones? Do ye?'

They move closer, miming an attack on the diggers, hands chopping up and down, punching and kicking. Although powerless to do the physical harm they wish to, they infest the air with a fearful sensation of horror. I steel myself against it; although, after all, they acknowledge me and can have no quarrel with such a harmless little pussycat as I.

When the more sensitive Tom looks around in fear the spirits cheer and renew their efforts. 'Can ye see yerself, my wee mannie? Digging up a poor lad from his grave? Ye'll be right sorry for this.' They are having some effect. Tom cowers and all but cries but Crowe remains oblivious. Jumping down into the grave with his impatience and frustration at Tom, Crowe begins to scrape dirt away with his hands. It is this one, the black-haired Crowe that really infuriates the spirits; they cannot reach him, he has little feeling. They would like to send him flying and see him cower in fear. They redouble their efforts to infest the air with dread, a soft keening blowing with the wind. They stare at me, as if this is my fault. I want to tell them that it is not me, and of course I cannot, but I feel so uncomfortable that I take the hint, leave them to it, and go back to Isla's grave.

It seems colder here, as if the winter chill has already settled. I am curled up, doing my best to keep warm, when, like a leaf floating on a gentle breeze,

Duncan Abernathy slowly descends to the burial ground, finally settling near his old grave, next to his wife's new one and almost on top of me. He seems to not quite perceive what is happening to him, he looks confused. He has come a long way, but how? I'd like to know that, too. But I am glad for Isla's sake that he is here. His confusion does not worry Duncan overmuch for his heart is peaceful. Other spirits move about him, looking at him with interest and I am there too, looking on and wondering. I always liked Duncan. He was a fair man, even if he chased me out of the back of his shop more times than I can count (if he could find me, that is). He preferred me to be in the kitchen, and to tell the truth, so did I. But back to my tale. The burial ground becomes more desolate, a place of sorrow for the living. The dead do not sorrow; those spirits that are left behind are merely waiting, patiently or not. Restless souls still walk here. As he comes to rest, Duncan watches the the darkness deepen and spread. Spirits greet him and some he knows, some he remembers. But where is Isla? It makes me sad to see his peaceful heart begin to worry. With some of his old friends here to greet him, it would almost be jovial to be here, if he didn't feel so strongly that Isla should be here. Where is his wife? He gazes thoughtfully at Isla's fresh headstone where I sit, waiting.

Isla Marie Abernathy
Beloved wife of Duncan
Born 1750 – Died 1833

Resting with God

After a couple of hours, Duncan's mind has cleared a little. Actually, it is well after midnight when two men, living men, approach the place where Duncan sits, near me and with his back to Isla's gravestone; their conversation is in hushed whispers, but clearly audible to the hovering spirits.

'Constable's gone, Tom, no need to fret now.'

No need to fret? What does he mean, Duncan wonders. They drop their barrow right next to him, pulling out a shovel and a lantern. Duncan's thoughts are still in a fog, but abruptly he realises what is going on; these men are grave robbers. Why else would they come here in the middle of the night? He starts alert in an instant. They are going to dig up Isla's coffin, his Isla's! 'Over my dead body!' he swears. I stifle a laugh!

'Dig, Tom, go on!' Crowe says, as he gives an uneasy glance around; he turns it into a shrug of bravado as Tom begins to throw up spadefuls of dirt.

Duncan manoeuvres himself to right above the grave; he uses all his will, all the power at his disposal, to infest the atmosphere with terror. This is when things start to heat up. He never knew he had such clout. Because it is new to him, he strains to do whatever can be done to discourage the diggers and send them flying. Surely he can frighten two foolish men, he thinks. He recognises that something is definitely happening within him. Still the spadefuls of earth are growing into a good-sized pile next to the grave as the men continue to dig.

Tom's spade strikes the wood of the coffin; he sees a faint nimbus in the hole he has dug and his eyes widen until the whites show all around. Duncan grins delightedly at his fear; he calls on whatever powers he has, feeling a righteous anger filling him.

Sensing this hostile presence, Tom trembles in horror, making the shovel rattle against the wooden casket.

'Ssh!' Crowe's anxious cry is itself too loud. He does not see the cloud around the coffin, but he sees clearly enough that Tom is terrified. His mate is getting more and jumpy on these jobs but Crowe has no one else he can trust. Quickly he lowers himself into the grave and tries to lift the coffin lid. It is heavy and awkward, but at last, it is off. And now, he sees that all is not well. Now he sees like Tom, that despite the clear night, a strange mist sits in the coffin obscuring the body. He steadies himself to take it, to be strong enough for Tom, strong enough for the two of them, aye and stubborn enough to finish the job. But I can see how he shakes right enough, even if Tom cannot.

'It's nothing, Tom, only a bit of mist. It's naught to worry over,' Crowe hisses.

'This is too much! You villains!' Duncan screams wildly, unheard by the two men, but the other spirits, riled up and prodded to give vent to an indignation they have been feeling for a long time, surround him and echo his words. They raise their fists and cry out;

and Duncan is the loudest. I realise that here is another one who needs me to look after him, now that
anger has taken hold. But, how am I to do it?

Crowe and Tom close their eyes and put their arms
through the mist. They heave Isla's body up and onto
the grass. Breathing unevenly, they are no less afraid,
but when Tom sees the glitter of gold on Isla's finger,
he grins. He forgets the white nimbus as quickly as he
was terrified by it a moment ago. He bends down, lifts
up poor Isla's hand and tugs at the ring.

'By God, do not take that ring! I'll have yer guts for
garters!' rails Duncan. I swipe at him vainly with my
good right paw and it's sharp talons, honed by me over
many hours for just such an occasion. Neither of us
do much good.

'No, Tom! Leave it. Don't take the ring,' unknow-
ingly Crowe echoes Duncan's words.

But Tom watches the gold shining in the lantern
light with a look of vacant delight. He pulls harder
and the finger breaks with a sharp crack as he falls
back. He pries off the ring and stares at it happily, as
it glows in his hand.

'Ye perfect loon!' growls Duncan.

'Look, Crowe! Look how it shines. Look how pretty
it is. Look.' Tom admires it before dropping it into his
pocket.

'Put it back, Tom.'

'I'll not,' Tom says, unsteadily. He does not know
what he is feeling, stubbornness or desire, anger or
fear, but he does not like it. He does not like con-

fronting Crowe. But he will keep the ring; the ring is a fine thing, and he has seen little enough of such articles. He will keep it in his pocket and feel it's perfect roundness, he will enjoy fondling it when no one knows what he is doing. He will feel grand with a piece of gold in his pocket and not a soul will know it is there, or what it means or what a fine fellow he is. It will be his secret. *Au contraire*, I think — all of us know it!

'I've told ye it's hanging for stealing jewellery. Put it back on her finger, Tom. Then Walters can deal with it.' Crowe tries to keep his voice calm but terror is eating into him. It is worse than the usual mild fear he experiences at being in the burial ground; his tough exterior is beginning to crack, the bravado that enables him to dig up dead bodies is fading. A nimbus hovers all around the body as well as within the coffin. Crowe ceases to speak, to think. He feels some forces gathering round him and his bowels turn to water. His watchful eyes no longer see anything, but stare with terror straight into nothingness.

The body stretches out on the ground, the two men at head and foot. Duncan hovers next to them, aware of the strangeness of something that is happening, not to them, but to him. Some power that is entering him, but whether good or evil he doesn't know; it is overwhelming just as it is. I fear for him, that if this is evil, I cannot protect him. Duncan has realized that these two idiots are stealing not only Isla's wedding ring, but her body as well. He is losing this battle and the knowledge fills him with an incandescent rage. He pours all his energy into terrorizing them and he can feel that unknown power growing in him. He can't comprehend what it is, but something is happening and the source of it is unknown. Somehow he has invited it in and despite its power he does not know if he likes it. Before he can think any further it possesses him, all of him, so that he cries aloud with the wild strength of it.

Looking in Duncan's direction Tom shivers, not from the chill wind that rattles the tree branches but from what he sees. Around him the gravestones are becoming lighter, changing slowly until they are as bright as the moon. They stand out glowing fiercely, each stone with a heart of fire that reaches out and hisses. I have seen this only once before, at a time of great change. Tom begins to shake as well he might. I am shaking a wee bit myself! 'They're here, Crowe. The ghosts are here!' But Crowe already knows. The fire and the hissing are nearing him. Scrabbling to his feet, Tom stands only to fall backward once again. In the trees the birds come to life, chattering with warning calls. The men grope in the darkness, the terror of each infecting the other.

Duncan feels shocked at the things he can do. He has power, aye, but it is stronger than him, it is overtaking him. He cannot control it, he cannot stop them in their crime, his will has been taken over completely, until in a heartbeat, like a light blown out, it is gone. Relief floods into him; it was too much, too strong for him and too menacing. He shudders as the aftershock leave him, sinking to the ground, hollow-eyed. Bit by bit his head clears, a feeling of tranquillity settles over him. There is a sense of something coming toward him, some revelation. He freezes. I circle around him, trying to slow him down, stepping deliberately one paw in front of the other, attempting to distract him. It does not work. Urgently, there is some action he needs to take, some important step he must initiate. We wait. Around him, the whirlwind slows to a feeling of drifting on a gentle ocean. Tom and Crowe, the other spirits, all recede into silence and darkness.

Before us we see two bright rings, Duncan's and Isla's, laying on the sacred cloth at their marriage ceremony. Sparks rise from them in a glittering, radiating force that pushes against us. We hear the preachers voice say, 'til death do us part.' Duncan feels the ring slide onto his finger and sees the deep wells of love and trust in Isla's eyes. Eyes so clear, with their specks of green and their dark rimmed irises, eyes with a depth that had captivated him all his days, that he begins to sink into them and . . .

Duncan snaps back to the now, and suddenly he knows what he must do to find Isla. It is all in their rings; the symbol of their union will bring them together again. Duncan must have his ring, and Isla must have hers. That is how they will find each other. The rings have the power to make sparks and the sparks are the force that will connect the rings. So with the rings' reunion, so too will he and Isla reunite. He rubs the worn gold band of his wedding ring, and sparks fly upward.

'Ahh, Belle,' he says, 'how beautiful, how braw it will be.'

Aye, but I see that Duncan has forgotten that Isla no longer has her ring. As memory dawns, he curses with a fine fury. 'Och, Belle, what can I do when Isla's ring is gone?' he demands of me and of course, I have no answer. Again the strange anger floods him, fills him; the gravestones burn and snap with the power of it, but this time he knows he does not like it, it must be controlled. It must be overcome or he may never get the ring back on his beloved's finger. That power is useless for what he wants. He cannot stop himself, he howls like a banshee, turns to the spirits behind him, and rushes through their midst, only to return a moment later.

Wildly, he lunges at Tom and falls straight through him.

Tom starts back, his face alight with horror. 'Crowe!'

'No one's here, Tom. There's no spirits.' Crowe's speech has taken on a coaxing tone, something to calm Tom, but Crowe too is frightened. He knows the spirits are here, knows that Tom is right. He fears the strange fog that plays around the casket. He just wants to get away, but unlike Tom, he knows that they cannot leave things as they are. 'Come on, just give me a hand to lift the body onto the cart. We'll put the ring back and . . . '

Tom sees more than Crowe; for Tom the grave-stones glow again with a terrible brightness, the terror is on him. 'Run, Crowe. I tell ye they're here! Do ye not see them? Look!' Tom points to the glowing lights coming from the tombstones; he hears the howling and at last he breaks and runs. Headlong down the path, Tom moves faster than he ever has in his life. The spirits convulse with laughter as he hightails it out the gate and down the road before the startled birds can even lift their feathers. Still with the ring in his pocket!

'Tom!' Crowe calls after him, louder and louder he calls. Crowe is desperate now for grave robbing is a two man job and already the sky seems lighter.

Duncan moves to hover directly before him as he croons over Isla's body.

Crowe does not see or hear him, but he feels the uncanny. His legs are moving before his brain knows of it. They pummel up and down with a life of their own and he is out of the burial ground and on the way to the Thistle in a heartbeat. All thought of the body and the ring, the commission from Dr. Walters, the danger to Tom, everything, everything is gone. He runs from pure terror.

The spirits have not had such a fine show in ages and they laugh and jest together over the finer parts for ages. Duncan, close by his wife's grave, rubs his ring over and over, watching the sparks arise. 'The sparks are for ye, Isla, but ye are not here. The ring is stolen,' he cries. 'I can do nothing for ye, my darling.

All the sparks in the world will not bring ye here to me! Why has this happened? Why has the ring been taken away? Why does cruel fate keep us apart? I canna bear this business.'

I consider. If she could, if all was well, if it was not for the two villains who have robbed him blind, Isla would be with Duncan now. They are still married; their love is strong. But now all is ruined. How can I tackle this mess?

Duncan curses Tom and Crowe with all of the power of his invention. Together we stay by the body until the sky to the east is filled with the light of morning, waiting for someone to discover the crime.

It does not take long.

29 October

Isla's narrative

The quiet seems to stretch out from the bones of the house itself, lingering as if the day hasn't yet begun, as if the sadness will last through years and years of waiting, and noise and life may never return. In the kitchen I watch where she stands as still as a statue in front of the window; her beautiful eyes are blank with an inward look. The leaves that have turned to red and gold litter the ground more than they decorate the trees. Their colours and fluttering do not distract her. Now is such a pretty time for Edinburgh, built as it is of the grayest of stones. People who pass by wear bright plaids and call greetings to each other. That feeling of life, of stirring with the day, is what I missed most of all when I was lying day after day in that blessed bed.

Charlotte moves more fully into the sun as it comes with a dull shine through the window. Bustling in with her hands full of laundry, Hannah turns to Charlotte with a smile.

'Hannah, I have set a date for the wedding.' Charlotte speaks in a rush.

Och! No!

' I want it to be soon, for I do not feel settled. It is to be the seventh of November at the Canongate Kirk.' She sounds nervous, as if she expects Hannah to disagree with her. 'We'll have a small wedding breakfast here afterwards.'

Hannah is caught off guard. 'Aye. An' I hope ye will be verra happy,' she says, her voice soft and soothing, but I know she is as unhappy as I am about it.

'Thank ye. I will not like to leave here.' The smile she calls forth is a poor thing and she trembles as she embraces Hannah. 'I feel both happy and sad.'

Och! It can't be happening, not with that poor excuse for a man, that puffed up bag of bones that thinks it is a fine gentleman. Nay, I will go through the gates of hell to stop their union.

'There, there,' murmurs Hannah, holding her close. 'Well, and where will you go? Yon Mr. Luke has nowhere but a hired room.'

'I don't know; we have not discussed it. He tells me not to fret at all. I'm sure he will have made some plans, Hannah.'

Oh, the foolish child!

'Aye, my chick — but still!'

'I know! I know! Och! so much has happened, and is happening verra quickly.' A wee frown appears between Charlotte's eyebrows.

How would they feel if they knew I could hear all of their chat? Would they speak differently? I wish I knew, but I don't think they would. So far I have been merely listening, hoping something will happen to stop this wedding. Now I feel like rattling a few pots and pans, throwing a few plates at the wall. Aye, I would if I could! But I will nay let her marry that Luke Harker, whatever! The man is a fraud; I don't know how or why, but he is!

As if to interrupt and force all to stop and think, Belle, stalking on her long legs, wanders into the kitchen, innocently waving her tail. Charlotte stoops down, picks her up and holds her close. 'Could Belle have been in my room last night?' she asks, stroking her fine fur. 'I'm sure I felt her jump up on my bed, stretching and fretting like mad, yet I am just as certain that I had closed my door.'

'Well, ye know the northerly was fair roaring last night. Perhaps it was a dream,' Hannah suggests. "Or a spirit.'

I stare at Belle.

'Perhaps,' says Charlotte. 'But it was so real. She

cuddled up to me and after I put my hand on her fur, she started purring, just like now. I went back to sleep then.' She runs her hand slowly over Belle's back and out along her tail. The cat settles further into her arms as if she can never settle deep enough and rests her head on Charlotte's forearm. 'But when I woke up the door was closed, and Belle was not there.'

"Well, it does not signify. Remember, Samain is soon,' says Hannah.

'And do we dream of cats at Samain?' Charlotte teases.

'Who knows? Cats also die.'

'Aye, perhaps it's true that animals have spirits. But Samain frightens me this year. The ghosts and haunting have always been jolly, but now I feel as if something terrible may happen. Oh, Hannah, how I miss my grandma!'

'Och, my dear, so do I. And it surely is a fearsome time.' Hannah comforts her, as she looks up at Mr. Muir, who has just come in. 'People forget that in all the excitement.'

'Forget what?' he asks, looking around him and warming his hands by the fire.

'They forget that Samain can be dangerous,' Hannah says stoutly. 'They forget that we light the bonfires for a verra good reason; that the fires guide the spirits of the dead so that they become visible to our poor human eyes. Aye, so that we can see them, so we know they are real. And by the bonfires we help open the gateway to the Otherworld.'

'Aye, that's how it is,' Mr. Muir agrees. *'Aye, people forget; they forget that the spirits may mingle with the living and we who are alive may not even know it. We may see them or we may not. We may see some and not others. We do not know the way of it at all.'*

'But I have always enjoyed it so!' exclaims Charlotte. *'It was always fun to go with Grandma and see the bonfires and the people. Was I wrong, then? Is it really a terrible time?'*

'Why, it is fun for the bairns, and a fine night, but along with the fun it is actually a verra serious business,' Hannah continues. *'All may mix at Samain, all, the living with the dead. The dead may visit the living. And what can that mean?'* Hannah begins to shudder with her own story. *'Would ye be there and find yerself mingling with a spirit, talking to one? Or waltzing with a spirit to a fine tune? For ye would not know, not know at all, until your partner vanished in a puff of air.'*

Och, I like to hear Hannah talk of Samain. I did not find Duncan at the Calton Burial Ground, nay, and the night of Samain may be my last chance. If ever I am to find him it will be tonight in that crowd of spirits, aye and find him I must. I'll not go through eternity without the wee bugger!

'Ah, Hannah! Then do you blame me for feeling frightened?' Charlotte asks.

'But why be afraid of the Otherworld, if you have done no sin?' Mr. Muir sees Charlotte's vulnerability in this conversation now, so soon after Isla's death. *'Why should any spirit harm you? They will not. Surely it is a*

time that you may see your grandma as she has passed so recently. And maybe e'en Duncan; I'd give a lot for that! And what a boon that would be to ye, for sure and certain.' His earnest eyes search her face. 'Just think on that.'

I like the lad more than ever; he is every inch the man he should be, but Charlotte will not be comforted.

'Ye have scared me, now! Aye, that ye have.' She throws her hands to her head and runs from the room.

Belle's narrative

Duncan is restless; he has been mourning over Isla's body all night while I have done my rounds. And when I return, tired and verra hungry, and perch once more on the headstone, watching, waiting, he rubs his ring to see a shower of sparks rise and burst. It does nay matter now. Her ring is gone. He knows full well that it is fruitless but keeps on, if listlessly, over and over again, his face looking baffled.

'Well, my bonny,' he says to me, 'surely she will be about on Samain; she will be among the spirits, riding the wild night air. Isla would never miss such a thing. And she, poor hen, will wonder where I am. Och, why is this so difficult? She is looking for me, I'm sure of it; she must be, for it is deep in her nature.' A pity I canna talk to him. I'd tell him that Isla is out there somewhere, and that he will find her, even if she has no ring, even if she cannot see him, even if all ways are barred. She will be looking for him; that is sure and certain. But I am only a cat, who cannot speak. Rising, he leaves the burial ground and heads up toward the Old Town and his shop, and I at his heels.

Through the windows, we see John Muir, Duncan's old apprentice, working in the Apothecary, while Charlotte, still a wee bit pale, and Hannah, are making oatcakes in the kitchen and chatting as they always did. I long to leave him, it was a long night, and look, there is the warm hearth that I like so much.

But there, sure enough, he sees his wife and I ken there will be no rest for me.

'Isla!' he calls, as I rub myself against his insubstantial leg.

Isla looks around uneasily. Again there is that feeling of a blanket falling about us. Something has pressed into the air around her, something she feels, but it is vague and uncertain.

'Isla, it's Dunc. I am come for ye!' He rubs his ring and the sparks fly and I move away. They are a grand sight, but I dinna like them burning my coat. Isla appears even more troubled, but it is clear that she sees nothing, hears nothing, and only feels that which cannot be defined.

'Belle, what can I do?' Duncan calls to me as I stare at him, as if he was a tender morsel of bird suddenly appeared on a platter just for me. I am so hungry I am hallucinating! I'd like to go to Isla, but it's no good. I canna leave Duncan just now. So I just meow in a low tone and make a beeline for the kitchen and the bowl of milk I hope will be sitting there for me. Ahh!

Mr. Muir is in the process of measuring out an ounce of fool hazel for a customer when the door opens and the Sheriff enters. After waiting for the young lady at the counter to be served and to leave, the Sheriff says in his quiet baritone, 'I'd like to speak to Miss Charlotte Ryan, sir, if she's about.'

Worried but obliging, Muir steps to the sitting room door and in a moment Charlotte comes hurrying out, followed by Hannah; and Isla.

'What is it?' she asks, a trifle sharpish.

'I'm sorry to bring you this news, Miss Ryan.'

No one addresses Charlotte as Miss Ryan. It makes her shy away from his serious look and deep voice as he asks, 'Would you like to sit down?'

Mr. Muir helps Charlotte to a chair, looking just as worried as Charlotte herself, and Hannah takes a seat beside her.

'Your grandmother's grave has been disturbed, Miss.'

At the Sheriff's words, Hannah cries out in horror.

Charlotte holds herself very still, one hand clasped tightly in Hannah's as she reaches out blindly with the other, where it is taken and held carefully by Mr. Muir. All three stare at the Sheriff who, seeming none too comfortable with his duty, swallows and clears his throat. 'Her body has been dug up. The warden found it lying on the ground next to her grave.'

Hannah and Charlotte grasp each other with even more fierceness.

'Such sacrilege! Such wicked men! And just before Samain,' Hannah rages.

Mr. Muir, eyes on Charlotte, looks distraught.

'On, on the ground?' Charlotte repeats in disbelief.

Isla stiffens. Duncan moves closer to her. 'Isla,' he says gently. 'Isla, can ye nay hear me?' But she does not, does not even know he is there. But she gives me a wee nod.

'It appears the robbers were disturbed before they could remove the body.'

And how they were disturbed! Duncan grins and as we exchange glances I smile like the old Cheshire cat.

'We believe a piece of jewellery has been stolen,' continues the Sheriff, 'which is a criminal offence. Miss Ryan, can you confirm that Mrs. Abernathy was wearing her wedding ring when she was buried?'

Isla looks down at her hand, surprised. Her ring is not there.

'Aye, it was the only jewellery she wanted.' Charlotte pauses, and continues in a weak voice. 'She is still there, lying on the ground?'

'Don't worry, Miss,' the Sheriff says as gently as possible. 'She will be reburied immediately. I will escort you to the burial ground now 'if you wish. Pastor Furphy has been sent for.'

'Aye, aye at once,' Charlotte cries, and she and Hannah run out in their shawls, the Sheriff coming behind. Mr. Muir rushes after them cradling Charlotte's warm coat in his arms but all are away and gone down the street. As Muir must stay behind to manage the shop and cannot leave, Dunc and I stay by him for a moment and watch the others hurry fast away. Muir's face is full of anguish and his eyes glassy with unshed tears. This is tricky for me – I know he is horrified about Isla's body, but I fear he is even more worried about Charlotte catching a cold, his not being close to comfort her.

'Such is love,' says Duncan. We go.

A small crowd has gathered behind Constable Dundee, who stands guard over the body, as they come running up. Pastor Furphy takes Charlotte's hand and begins to pray. As a holy man, I wonder if he can feel the eyes of Isla and Duncan on him. Now that Isla's only relative is here, the pastor gives a small signal to a workman, who lowers himself into the grave and stands with his legs apart on either side of the open coffin; he accepts the body carefully from another who stands above him. Arranging Isla's body once more in the coffin, he is very gentle and careful with everyone looking at him. Charlotte does not take her eyes away from her grandmother and the ringless finger that hangs at a strange angle. The body is so pitiable, so devoid of everything that made Isla her grandmother that suddenly her gorge rises; she knows she will be sick, and turns away into the bushes. She gags on her bile, not having eaten much that morning.

'Is there no end to the world's wickedness? What sort of person would dig up an old lady?' She cries.

'Aye, my lass, aye, it is an evil world to be sure, with no end of wickedness in it.' Hannah brings out her handkerchief, gently wiping Charlotte's face and making soft murmurs in her ear until she is calm. Hannah is good at this sort of thing. Sometimes I sit in her lap just for the comfort of it.

Charlotte twists the engagement ring that her grandma gave her such a short time ago; twists it round and round. The casket lid makes a dull scrape as it is fitted back onto the wooden frame and nailed into position. As Pastor Furphy begins to recite the Prayer for the Dead, Luke Harker arrives. As if she has been drowning, Charlotte reaches for him and on being in his arms, she breaks out in a wail. Luke embraces her, but not without first brushing his hands over his coat, tidying his appearance. A dandy. Not one of us, apart from Charlotte, likes Luke and it seems so wrong for him for him to be here. I feel angry tension emanating from Duncan. No one speaks as the men shovel the earth into the grave until it looks as it did before.

Charlotte searches for Hannah's eyes. 'I was right to be afraid,' she says.

This prompts me to relive the wild doings of the previous night; Duncan's ire at seeing the robbers, his rough rage and the glowing of the stones. Even though I was there, it seems unreal and I wonder how he will reach Isla. There must be a way, but still it is a mystery. His eyes are always on her. How will he control that wild power that he seems to command? And oh Lord, how will we keep her safe, if bodies are to be dug up willy nilly?

My heart goes out to Charlotte and I remember that this is Duncan's first sight of his granddaughter in a long time. She is a beautiful young girl, but her naivety and need shine out clear. Also it is his first sight of Luke Harker — not reassuring!

Duncan turns to me and says, 'Yon loon I do not like. He reminds me of a customer that I had when I was just starting out. It was a young man, no older than me, who declared it was urgent; his mother needed the medicine or she would die. He solemnly swore to pay as soon as he could. Aye, he was convincing with his desperate look and eyes so ready to weep. And like enough it was true. I gave him the mixture but the man never returned. It was an expensive mix and cost me dearly. I lost money at a time when it really mattered, at the very beginning of setting up shop.' He pauses and sighs heavily, then stares hard at Luke before resuming.

'That was a lesson I still remember well, and yon fine peacock is the image of that man. Aye, this Luke has something of his manner and presence; too plausible by half, something of the dissembler about him, only made worse by his fancy suit and foolish handsome face.'

I nod. I am no friend of Luke, he makes me want to vomit. I wonder if Luke may even have had something to do with the theft of the ring. He seems the type that would not get his own hands dirty, but would not be above a wee spot of skulduggery if it were to his profit. I can tell from the way Hannah speaks of him that she does not like Luke Harker and I have always been in awe of her sixth sense, especially when it comes to the seamier side of Edinburgh.

Luke starts to usher Charlotte toward the gate with most of the crowd following.

Duncan says softly, 'I'm going to follow that bugger. If I can't get through to Isla, I will try to look out for Charlotte, at least until Samain begins.'

When I've had a bit of shut-eye and something to eat, I go down to the Thistle for a little quiet, after all the goings on. Beneath the trees on the side of the street opposite the pub I see Tom and Crowe arguing. Turning away and pulling the ring from his pocket, Tom commences grinning and running back and forth under the bare branches to see the dappled light on the fine gold band that gleams in the sun. He does look like a daftie if ever I saw one.

'Put it away, Tom. Do ye not remember how ye saw the spirits? Are ye not a' feared?'

Seeming not to hear him, Tom tilts the ring this way and that, admiring its shine.

'You know you will hang if they find it on you,' Crowe tells him.

'I'm hungry,' Tom says, spinning the ring on his palm. 'Can we go into the pub?'

'No, Tom! It isn't safe, did nay I tell ye? It is discovered. The body has been found!'

'Found?!' Tom gapes. 'But, we tried to put it back. We had to leave it! Ye saw how the tombstones were afire, hissing and glowing with the faery light. The spirits were a'hauntin last night. Ye saw it, Crowe, ye did!'

'I know, I know. But the body is found and we, we should nay be here. The law is a'lookin for that ring.'

Reluctantly Tom drops the ring into his pocket. Hitching up his pants and swiping at his nose with the back of his hand, he blinks his eyes in dull resentment. 'Well, Sandy's all right, isn't he?' he asks.

Oh, God, what a perfect boob he is!

'He said he'd buy it. He said I was too scared to do it, but I wasn't, was I Crowe?' Tom asks happily. 'I took it, didn't I, last night? I was brave, brave!'

'Aye, ye were a fine fool last night,' Crowe replies in a flat tone.

'Sandy's in the pub now - let me go in Crowe! Can I? He'll give me good coin for it.'

'No! Good coin! He'll give ye naught but trouble. Tom, we've been lucky. You can't sell it to Sandy, not to anyone. You can't even show it to anyone! Don't go and get yourself hanged.'

Tom stares at his feet, his hand still in his pocket. 'I won't get caught.'

'The Sheriff is hunting for that ring. There is sure to be someone that will snitch if you try to sell it. You can't trust Sandy. '

'You don't know everything, Crowe! Sandy's my friend,' Tom says stubbornly.

'Sandy is nobody's friend but his own!' Crow looks desperate. He may well be convinced of the reality of the ghosts and their power after last night, for he says, 'Besides, the spirits want that ring back!'

Tom hops from foot to foot. He looks at the pub like it is his lost love. Before Crowe can stop him he is off. I am torn between going with Tom, and staying with Crowe, but it looks as if the action will be in the pub.

'Tom!' Crowe calls, but does not follow. His cry is lost in the banging of the pub door.

In the Thistle Sandy grins his wolf's grin as he sees Tom come in. His smile widens as Tom looks around him. Sandy rises so that Tom can see him and moves into the greater darkness of a corner so that Tom follows, almost skipping with anticipation. They greet; Tom pulls the ring from his pocket and shows it to Sandy proudly, talking fast, telling him the tale of last night, gesticulating with his hands. Sandy waits until he is done before he begins to laugh. 'Ah Tom, I canna take it. Ye were a fool to steal from the dead.' At first Tom looks confused but then his face darkens.

I hate the man with his snaky red hair and cruel ways; he looks at Tom the way I sometimes look at a herring in my bowl.

Sandy laughs harder, taking little punches at Tom, knocking him round the head, and nearly choking with glee. Tom suddenly takes a swipe at Sandy, but misses and falls onto the floor; rage jumps into his eyes. He scrambles up and Sandy is crowing like a rooster as Tom leaves the Thistle, running from the sound of his mirth, his catcalls, and back to Crowe.

'He laughed at me, Crowe,' he blurts out. 'After all that, he wouldn't even buy it, after he promised! The bastard.' Tom kicks at the stones on the road. 'I'm going back to Calton,' he gasps, pulling out the ring, 'to put it back.'

Tom is already moving and Crowe races to catch him. 'Nay, nay, not now, Tom! It's broad daylight. Not now, we'll do it tonight.'

Tom slows his pace. 'He laughed at me, laughed and laughed. It's bad luck, Crowe. The ring, I mean.' He looks down, looks everywhere but at Crowe. 'Bad luck for Samain! It itches in my pocket. Bad mebbe for hanging.' Stumbling, Tom lets his head drop forward.

'It'll be all right, Tom. We'll do it tonight!' Crowe glances furiously toward the pub, his hands bunched into fists. 'Tonight, in the dark,' he says.

'Alright!' Tom blinks. 'That bastard! I'll get him, Crowe! You wait; I'll get 'im. It's his fault, everything, the spirits too. He's the one who lied.' Tom seems to have calmed down some, and Crowe looks relieved.

They are waiting for night after all. Thank God! These energetics are wearing me out. They move slowly away from the pub and to their poor lodgings, where they do nothing until night time I suppose. Nothing for me to do now but wait, so I take a moment to catch my breath, and head to the other part of town, to the solicitor's.

Luke and Charels work at their respective desks, each a picture of industry, smiling to themselves like a couple of cats that have gotten into the cream and aren't letting it go any time soon. I settle down to listen and am nearly asleep when I see Duncan drift down into the room. He looks around and finds a space. He has been here before, of course. He made out his will here with old McCormack, as well as tending to other business matters, but since then Jenkins is gone and taking his place is the new man, Luke Harker, the man he saw take his granddaughter into his arms. I can't blame him for looking angrily at Luke in his fine suit as his pen scratches across the paper, but Luke keeps his eyes down, robbing Duncan of any chance to see into them.

Looking grim, Mr. McCormack opens his door and enters the main office. 'I have all the figures from the past three months, gentlemen, and I'm off to give them to my accountant,' he says. 'The figures do nay look good at all and I will get to the bottom of this, ye can be sure.' He looks at Harker and Charels with a stony eye. 'If ye have anything to say before I go, ye'd better say it now.'

Duncan and I exchange raised eyebrows. Now Duncan knows that it's something about money; I should have known, his eyebrows say - Luke must have his finger in a pie somehow.

'But there's nothing wrong, sir,' says Luke. 'I've been through it again. It all balances. See here.' Endeavouring not to look worried, he raises the ledger. 'It tallies, all of it!'

Duncan laughs.

Charels supports Luke with a vigorous nod.

'Nothing wrong,' Luke repeats.

'He's guilty as hell,' whispers Duncan.

'Is that all ye have to say?' asks Mr. McCormack. 'Charels?'

'I am sure the figures add up, sir. Come, we can go through them now.'

'I've been through 'em well enough.' Mr. McCormack speaks deliberately. 'I don't know how it's being done, but something is amiss. I've been doing this long enough to know when I'm being diddled and I won't have it. No, sir! Mr. Silver will accompany me on my way to find out what is going on.' He glares at them. 'Silver!' he bellows.

Silver comes running out from the back. 'Aye sir, Mr. McCormack.'

'Ye'll come along with me, laddie.'

Excited to be getting out of the office, Silver quickly struggles into his jacket.

'Well, this is your last chance,' McCormack announces, scowling at the other two.

Neither Luke nor Charels speaks; they dare not look at each other, each trying to hide his dismay.

Old McCormack treats them to another angry stare before he exits out the door, Silver close on his heels.

'We are so close,' Charels says hoarsely.

The conspirators look at each other with worried faces. I move closer.

The room falls into silence.

'This has something to do with Charlotte, I'll wager,' Duncan growls.

I nod. It has to be.

Later, Harker trudges back home to his lodgings with the visible me and the invisible Duncan beside him; Luke gives me a wee kick when he thinks no one is looking, the silly baboon. He moves with shuffling steps, always looking down at his feet. Like me, Duncan must be loathing the feel of the man, the lack of substance. Once in his bedroom, Luke grabs the whiskey before even taking off his coat. Lifting the bottle, he salutes the room with a gesture. 'Sl'ainte!' Sitting on the end of the bed, staring at nothing, he is jittery, afraid.

Duncan looks around the room. 'Well, am I going to learn anything at all here? Look at this — all these papers on the desk covered in figures, but I can't make much of it.' He hangs there waiting until Luke goes to his portmanteau and pulls out a couple of envelopes. Gliding over as the first letter unfolds, he leans over Luke's shoulder. The letter is a good fortnight old and sitting on the bed, as near to Luke as I dare, I read it along with them.

London, October 15th 1833

Dear Mr. Edwards,

I trust your contribution will soon be complete. The money received so far is safe and ready to be invested as arranged in United Sugarcane of Jamaica. The shares at present are worth little, as you must know, but your money combined with my own will make up an investment of so many shares that my head is spinning. Although impatience is goading me, I will wait for the wedding with its attendant final contribution, before I begin to buy up shares in a discreet manner. I shall then put it about that the sugar market is ready to soar and that the supreme winner in this surge will be United Sugarcane of Jamaica. I am delighted at the thought of it. My business contacts are extensive, as they include some of my Parliamentary colleagues, and my advice in business matters is well-respected. My well-known connection to the King also serves to boost my own credibility. With my record thus far unblemished, I will be believed, I have no doubt. The rumour should spread like wildfire. I trust that the news of a sugar boom will appear in the Times and the Observer without delay. By my estimation, in little over a month we should be able to sell at double our original investment.

As soon as I receive your final instalment, the last of the shares will be bought under your current alias of Luke Harker. It is a pity this deception is required, but, as you must be only too well aware, a warrant for your arrest is still current; you will be glad to hear that from what I can gather the authorities continue to believe that you are already out of the country.

I also consider it to be a pity regarding your betrothed. However, it is of the utmost necessity and importance that the young lady in question continue in ignorance until you and Charels are safely away in Johannesburg.

Keep me closely informed of events. Be as quick as you can. I need not remind you that the most urgent secrecy is to be observed. BURN THIS LETTER as soon as you have read it.

Yours in quiet collaboration,

R. Sherringham

Duncan begins to swell in an appalling manner. I too am horrified, but I cannot help noticing what a very poor conspirator Luke is. He had not burnt the letter as he was instructed to do, and here it is in his room for anyone to see. We are both looking at Luke with disgust when, with a sigh, he opens the second letter written in a softer hand, and spreads it open on the desk beside the first.

Johannesburg, September 6th 1833

My dearest husband Luke,

    I have missed you sorely and the children are asking when their father is coming home to them . . .

'You villain!' Duncan hisses in Luke's ear, wilder than a winter storm. 'You will pay for this!' His incandescence fills the room. I am glad to see Luke abandoning the letter, shrinking into himself. I am glad that Duncan has some power in him. Oh, but this is worse than I thought! Worse than anything! Poor Charlotte, that dear child.

Later that evening I sit watching Dr. Walters waiting at his window, his pensive eyes studying the dark street. There is no movement there, no noise. It is Edinburgh at its densest, it's most arcane; not even a dog is howling. It is so bleak that I leap to the doctor's window ledge and meow as piteously as I can until he opens up and lets me in. I go with him as he turns back to his desk and rereads his notes.

'Flora Ferguson

Skin has become translucent. Breathing is laboured, cough producing blood. Still eats, but very little. She is sustained by her father's visits only. As was the case with her mother, her consumption is the result of poverty, cold, poor hygiene, hard work and poor diet.'

I watch him as he raises his hands and sinks his head heavily into them. The crackling of the fire sounds bitter, and the reflection of its flames in the whiskey bottle dance with the brightness of Lucifer himself.

'Give me a body, just one more,' the doctor says into the empty room. "Pray God, just one more, or Flora will be dead in days.' I feel for the man, he is burning himself up with longing. For the remainder of the night he prays, drinks whiskey and waits at the shadowy window, while I doze and watch.

30 October

Belle's narrative

The morn is bonny and fine, and I trot along homeward feeling at peace with the world. I spy Duncan drifting up the road toward his old Apothecary's shop. He hails me and waits as I come up, all the while rubbing his wedding ring, idly watching the sparks. Poor man, even these seem dull to him for there are no answering sparks from Isla. All around his old home he hovers; he looks into the shop and nods to himself as he sees the careful way Mr. Muir serves his customers. Hannah and Charlotte, clearly visible through the window, make bread, kneading and shaping it into careful loaves. Duncan reaches out his hands. I ken that he has the imagination to think it would be nice, even after all this time, to taste some of that bread again. Like him, Isla, who is within, watches the goings on in the kitchen, and Duncan calls to her, 'Isla! Isla!'

She does not react and he shouts again 'Isla, I'm here.' Instinctively, he reaches again for his ring; sparks cascade upward but Isla merely looks around as if searching for something. 'Can ye not see me, my darling?' Duncan cries. 'Oh, look, look at the sparks I am making.'

But of course Isla cannot see him; she needs her ring for that. A troubled expression crosses her face; something seems wrong. She mutters, 'now, Duncan my lad, where are ye?'

'Uh!' Duncan looks as if he would enjoy kicking something just now, if he had a proper foot. I can't help a wee laugh.

Isla spies about her and sees nothing amiss, just Hannah and Charlotte at work in the kitchen, just me lying on the window sill, just me stretching, standing up and rotating my head. I blink my eyes slowly and look straight at Duncan, hoping she will follow my gaze. Something trembles in the air around us. 'Belle?' she asks. 'Can ye feel it too?'

I answer with a purr. Duncan meanwhile stares in unhappy disbelief. I know that this is the moment he has been waiting for, for so long. 'Here we are, both together, yet nothing!' he grumbles. 'What new punishment is this? Why can she not see me? Oh, my bonny Isla, I'll see ye get your ring back, somehow!' With a bitter expression, he wafts away, away from his old home and his wife. I, too, am on my way out the window. Isla will have to wait. Duncan and I are heading back to Calton Burial Ground.

Standing next to Isla's grave, once more a neat and tidy mound of earth, Duncan seems both lost and angry. I would like to distract him, or to make everything alright again, one or the other. Of course, I have no power of my own, I can only be an observer in the natural course of things. Still, it seems I ought to try. In one smooth movement I leap from a standing start to the top of Isla's headstone, stretch, and neatly fold myself into a lying position. We remain there the whole day through. Comes the darkness and still we sit. I gaze tiredly at Duncan with my magical topaz eyes (so I've been told — excuse me the vanity), but he is not looking at me; he is watching with a mixture of fury and horror at two familiar figures approaching from the distance.

Oh God, this is just what we need! Why are they here at the very start of Samain, surely an unpropitious time for mere mortals to be messing with the dead? Duncan begins to breathe hard; they must be here to dig up another body — even after the fiasco and terror of two nights ago. They should have been scared off for months, yet here they are, as bold as brass! The black sky with no moon mists over the ground as they come up close to him, right over Isla's grave. Duncan rounds on them, 'Get away! Get away!'

Tom starts back. Haha! Duncan is getting through.

'Aye,' says Isla's husband. 'And now what is it, ye black hearted villains? Back to the same grave? Did I not scare ye witless last time?'

I am too frightened to watch him; he has become dangerous again. Does he know his power?

I hiss, leaping at the two grave robbers and baring my claws; why make it easy for them? Although Tom cowers, Crowe tosses me out of the way, but I let loose with a demon's scream and try again. 'Good girl,' Duncan hisses. 'Come on, again!' But I've no mind for it. I've recalled that Tom wants to return the ring, the very thing that Duncan wants, but I've no way to tell him. He seems to be boiling with rage.

While Tom paces back and forth clutching that troublesome ring, Crowe picks up the old spade and pierces the ground.

'Hurry, hurry. I am a feared,' Tom whispers harshly.

'Stay stout, Tom.' Crowe digs in silence while Duncan circles him, cursing under his breath.

'I've got it. Give me the ring,' Crowe says.

Duncan falls back in confusion, the truth still eluding him. 'Ah, the ring! Aye, Aye. What of the ring?'

Handing Crowe the ring, Tom jumps down into the hole and together they begin heaving at the lid. But it is nailed on hard this time, and no amount of pushing and pulling will loosen it.

Crowe reaches into his inside pocket and pulls out a claw hammer.

'Damn ye, get oot the way!'

It takes a while and a great deal of cursing before the lid is loose enough to pry off.

Tom looks around him at the myriad of gravestones and as he does so, he shakes and closes his eyes. So he should too, if he remembers how they glowed the night before. Lucky for him that Duncan, confused but hopeful and watching intently, reins in his anger. He tries to not even look at his wife's mutilated body, not wanting to cause any inadvertent disturbance.

'Just get the ring on, Crowe, that's all,' urges Tom.

"I see, I see! Grand! That's it, get that ring on. Get it on and be gentle, ye young morons!' Duncan coos with delight.

Crowe tries to force the ring onto her finger, but the hard ring and the hard and broken finger rub against each other, resisting his efforts. He stops often to look over his shoulder; the night is as black as ebony. He grunts and mutters, twisting the ring. He pushes harder; the finger is already broken but still it will not slide on. Eventually with a terrible scratching sound, the small gold ring slides over the knuckle, pulling off poor Isla's pitiful dead skin, until it is back where it belongs.

I let out a soft purr. Duncan looks elated, relieved. Still I sense that he remains in a cold fury from the night Crowe and Tom dug up the body, disrespectful of Isla, of the dead. The heat of his anger from that night seems to have gone, but not entirely. It has turned to deadly cold.

'Ye'll see me soon!' Duncan crows. 'It is Samain, ye know, I'll pay ye a special visit! Aye, the trouble ye have caused me!' He begins to swear and the mist begins to swell and move, but still it is an icy anger, and under Duncan's control. It is grand, the way he frightens them. Crowe and Tom work like madmen, filling in the grave at top speed, constantly looking into the darkness and beyond. Now other spirits crowd around, enjoying the reversal of their actions — not stealing from a grave, but returning something to it. I think perhaps some feeling of a sort of satisfaction, of justice, fills them.

'Crowe, it's happening again!' Tom cries. 'Do ye feel it, man?'

Crowe, that man of cool sense and survival, feels it, feels the power of the unknown and fears it. The mound of the grave quickly rises, until at last, Tom and Crowe race away, disappearing as the sound of their running feet echoes back long after they are out of sight.

'That's grand, ma Belle, grand. Her wedding ring is back!' Duncan laughs and laughs and grins at us all.

Isla's narrative

Dark night, and the end of the day when Charlotte saw me buried for the second time. I watch as she undresses, carefully putting away her day clothes and laying out a fresh dress, the material covered with sprigs of heather that suit her complexion just fine, for the morning. Just as I taught her. Her pale skin reflects the glow of the firelight, beautiful in the darkness. I hover in the background, remembering Duncan and previous Samains we spent together; the fine times we had danc-

ing before the bonfires and looking at the moon, taking part in the letting go, the sensation of wild mayhem when ye knew that anything could happen, the general fear and fun combined. I want Charlotte to have some of that same fun, and that same awful awareness of the mystery beyond us. But it will not be now, I tell myself. Not now when she is so low, and outside her bedroom window the dark grey clouds sit, all mist, and barely move. A faint glow from scattered windows is the only light. It is not yet the time for her, but it will come.

Charlotte puts on her white nightdress and pulls down the gay bed-covers; I try to communicate some feelings of comfort, some ease and peace to the lassie. I feel our kinship surround us, our souls connect, but despite this awareness I have, Charlotte is all lonely. She runs the silver hairbrush, the one that I gave her for her 13th birthday, through her bonny locks. The poor child looks exhausted; she has not slept these past few nights. I have seen her lying awake, staring at the window, tossing and turning. My sharper senses, which still surprise me with their power, tell me she is thinking of the sight of my old body lying on the ground, my broken finger, and the dirt over my fine green dress and wrinkled face. I shudder for her, wishing it away, wanting to let her know I am fine.

'Grandma?'

The word startles me.

'Grandma, I hope you are at peace now . . .' I have to strain to hear her because her voice is verra weak and distant. 'I hope you are with grampa.'

'Aye, aye. I am at peace,' I say. 'God bless you child.' I wish I could tell her I am with her grampa too, but cannot. And I wish that I could tell her a bed time story to comfort her and take her mind off her troubles, as I did when she was younger.

But Charlotte has gone to sleep, numb with grief. I don't know if she hears me, or senses me. Hours I stay with her until she stirs again; as she slowly comes awake her face contracts. Bad memories crowd in on her again — I can feel it. Those cruel men who dug up my body, do they ever think of the consequences of their actions for others? Sacrilege! Again I wish I could rid her of those dreadful images of myself, all dirty and in that odd position, the broken finger. I am done with that old body, it does nay matter any more. But while I fill with anger, I ken how Charlotte grieves. My anger is not right; it will not gladden her and I must calm myself, but I always was a fiery bugger! Not like my granddaughter who has been a placid soul right from the beginning. Lighting her candle and rising from bed, Charlotte goes to the window and looks out. The branches of the tree move as slow as can be. No one is about. Helplessly I give her a ghostly kiss and after a time, she climbs back under the blankets and falls asleep.

Samain, 31st October 1833

Isla's narrative

At first light, I follow Charlotte down to the kitchen. The shadows under her eyes make her look older than her few years. Hannah is already working, moving slowly, but she gives Charlotte a smile and good morning.

'Good morning, Hannah! Will ye come to Calton Burial Ground with me? I want to lay some heather on the graves.' As she speaks she pours some tea from the pot and stirs in some milk. She passes it to Hannah. Ah, she is a kind child, thoughtful.

'Aye, I'd like to come.'

They look at each other bleakly.

'Do you think . . . could it be that . . .?' Charlotte's voice trembles.

'No!' Hannah says sharply, but quickly calms herself. 'No one has disturbed the grave again, of that I'm sure. We would know. For one, the sheriff would have told us by now. Yet I canna help wanting to tidy it after yesterday — and your grandpa's too; aye, and to lay some heather there. It will be a good start to the day.'

I nod my head like a daft wee bird that canna control its movements.

Belle's narrative

There is something I like about Samain. I like it's mystery, and it's religion. I love the way the air is crisp and cold, not at all like any other time of year. All through the day, men lay rushes for the bonfires, children play at ghostly games, screaming and pushing each other about, while women bake for the midnight feast. It seems a bonny holiday. This year a cloudy sky comes for Samain, shifting and moving until it settles in banks that seem to hover too close to the earth. As the sun sinks, leaving an afterglow of pinks and reds, more of the townspeople emerge from their houses or poorer dwellings, and make their way to the Royal Mile where bonfires are being lit. As darkness falls the crowd grows, full of noisy anticipation.

The people are afraid the spirits will come; I have heard many say so. And they are right, for drawn by the great fires, they do arrive, some searching, some lost and crying, some ready for mischief and misrule.

In the middle of the Calton Burial Ground bonfires snap and burn; townspeople mill around, visiting the plots of their dead, whose spirits surround them, hoping for any scrap of news, examining them for small changes, some eager for signs of ageing. Some of the ghosts call out respectfully to their relatives, others dance wildly. On Samain there are no rules and there is no uniformity. The spirits act as they will, and so do the living. Catching the light from the bonfire, gravestones and monuments take on an added layer of otherworldly eeriness on top of their grey cold hardness. There are many places I could be tonight (and will be later on), but for the now here I am. I generally come here in the early part of the evening on Samain because it is an important place and I need to know what is going on here before heading into town.

Mrs. McIver, at the headstone of her husband, prays and looks fearful. Dressed completely in black and with her high velvet bonnet sitting none too securely on her head she is a picture of propriety. It has been many years since Mr. McIver passed away. I wonder where he is, if he is here and can see her, if he can affect her. I am sure she hopes not; go to church she might, but she was nay a good wife. She closes her eyes as if to pray but she does not fully close her eyes. No, she watches everything through narrow slits between her lids; but still she does not see the dark figure of Sandy as he glides up behind her. I could give them both a shock now if I wanted — jump on Sandy's back or let out a wail — but I do not. I would rather see what happens. Silently Sandy's eyes examine the lady's cape and bonnet. His thin hand slowly moves forward, feeling gently along the cloak; thoroughly covering it all but finding nothing. Mrs. McIver, awake to the evils of thieves and cutpurses on such a night, clutches her small reticule tightly between her palms. This wee pantomime gives the spirits a good laugh and how I laugh with them! They love to see the manoeuvrings between rich and poor, now that they no longer take part. Sandy, defeated, slowly withdraws his hand, and he looks about for other rich people in the crowd. Seeing that it is mainly poor folk who are congregated here, he hurries away out the gate. We all know there will be many of the rich sauntering the Royal Mile; Samain always provides easy pickings there.

Mrs. McIver, when she has finished her fake and febrile prayers, walks forward in the direction of the open gate. Her mincing footsteps make quiet clicks on the path. The crowd of people ignores her, mesmerized by the blaze of the fire and the figures that leap and spin around it. The other crowd, the spirits, follow her.

'What are ye doin' here, ye old bat? Ye cared not at all for yer old man, worked him into the ground, did ye not?' asks one.

'You made my life a misery,' says another.

They move backwards in front of her, jeering and gesticulating, snapping their fingers in her face.

Although she sees none of them, she shivers. She turns back for a moment towards the grave of her husband and a tear runs down her cheek. 'I'm sorry,' she whispers.

The spirits laugh with a wild frenzy. 'Don't be sorry! It will do ye no good,' they jeer at the old woman. 'Ye will pay, aye, ye'll pay!'

As if a colder chill settles around her, she pulls her cloak tighter. That stout and dignified woman, that fine Mrs. McIver, begins to run. Her small feet, tightly encased in their buttoned-up boots, wobble as she hurries along.

'Ye'll pay,' the spirits howl. 'Oh, how ye'll pay!'

Children skip between the headstones, but are careful not to touch them. The older ones monitor the younger. The more solemn faces of their parents do not rejoice; they look anxiously at the headstones, at their neighbours and into the far distance. I feel a wave of dark vibrations, a sudden earnest fear. Do they feel it too? They can do nothing but stare at the bonfire as it leaps skyward sending up sparks that snap and fly.

No one notices when Mrs. McIver trips and falls at the iron railings of the gate and does not get up again. No one sees except the spirits, and they rejoice, surrounding her poor dead body, and beginning a long slow dirge as her ghost rises and looks anxiously around. They clap and mutter as they advance on her.

It is time for me to go to my next port of call on the Royal Mile.

It's true that there is always a deal of rough housing at Samain and a cat has to watch herself, not to be kicked or thrown into the fire, or set alight by some great wit. There are a million ways to torment us and some think this night gives them license to do whatever wrong they choose. So, especially here in the town, I am going to stay as quiet and inconspicuous as can be.

In the shadows I see Crowe and Tom standing and watching the mayhem.

The ghostly figure of Duncan stays close to them, watching the watchers.

Without any conscious thought, he falls to rubbing his ring and observing the sparks rise. And way over there, see Isla flit past, searching for Duncan but she cannot see him or his sparks. So there is no joy yet for them in this weird crowd made up of both the living and the dead. They have moved far apart before Isla rubs her ring and the sparks burn bright. But by that time Duncan has ceased rubbing his. They continue on, separate lonely entities adrift in the vast Edinburgh night.

On Princes Street the mayor, carrying a burning torch, moves forward with slow and self-important steps and tosses it into the highest stack of timber and pitch. The flames leap up against the utter blackness of the sky to the crazed dancing of the children and the cheering of the crowd. Wild with excitement, Tom rushes forward to join the children and begins jumping high in the air, spinning in an arc in the brief seconds between rising and falling. I fall back, determined to stay in the shadows. Tom's figure lit by the firelight is bizarre, mesmerising; the crowd oohs and ahhs, encouraging him to jump higher, to go nearer to the fire. Crowe gives a reluctant smile as he watches; although he sips his ale, his eyes do not leave Tom's frolics.

Duncan says, 'Och, Tom, ye'r naught but a poor wee fool, are ye not? Perhaps I do pity ye, after all.'

'Look at me, Crowe! Watch my capers!' Tom shouts while he dances. Light fizzes around his antics. The crowd cheers again.

Crowe raises his arm in a wave; he is almost happy. But his smile disappears when a nut red head of hair pops up beside him. A raspy persuasive voice asks,

'Have ye thought about my offer, Crowe? It will nay last forever.'

Duncan moves closer, the better to eavesdrop.

Crowe shakes his head. 'I told ye no; we do not want it. Get someone else.'

Sandy lowers his voice even more. 'Tom does not agree with ye, ye know.'

Slowly and deliberately Crowe turns and grabs Sandy by the jacket. 'Leave Tom alone.' He speaks just as softly. 'I swear ye'll be sorry if ye don't.'

Sandy laughs, pulling away with some force, as if he was ready for a stoush. 'Ye can't watch him all the time, ye know! I'll be reelin' in the wee daftie, ye watch me.' He waits, but Crowe only glares. 'This is worth a lot of gen to me.'

'Do you forget so soon? Ye would not buy his ring,' Crowe hisses. 'Tom wants nothing to do with you!'

'And what is this? What's been going on, ye nasty piece of goods?' Duncan rasps out.

Perhaps Sandy has heard this, or sensed some menace, for he gives a slight start. Crowe does not notice, but I do and am glad. Sandy backs into the crowd, his jabbing defiant voice floating over the top of it. 'It's him who forgets. Ah, Crowe, we're mates again, the best of mates, haha!' He moves slightly, is out of sight and lost in the crowd in a trice.

Eyes as bright as beacons, Tom runs back to Crowe. 'Did you see my dancing? Did ye, Crowe? I was up, up so high.' He jumps and gestures.

'Shut up! Shut up, will ye?' Crowe barks.

Tom flinches; his face turns red and he looks angrily at Crowe, but he is too excited to stop for long and goes racing back to the flames.

Duncan looks after him, then turns his attention to Crowe, who has begun to curse himself and his whole life.

'Dinna curse, man! Ye have a life, have ye nay? One day, ye'll be as me and able to do naught! Ye'll see how little all this with Sandy matters. The man is not your concern.' Duncan rages, trying to get through. 'Though ye may not know it now, what ye do with Tom is topmost, ye silly wee bugger! Your job is to look after Tom.'

Flasks are out for a wee dram. Many of the revellers were drunk before the night began. Under the raucous bravado of loud singing runs a vein of fear; it is an unknown night. Things happen on Samain that no one can explain. The year before last all the milk was spoiled, and the cows would not be milked for a week. It was a sad time for us cats, aye. The darkness sinks into a deeper black. Dread excites the watchers. Kenny Silver has brought his fiddle and the children dance and jig to his airs. Those who have come in disguise move stealthily among the crowd, enjoying their anonymity. A game of tossing apples has begun. Acrobats tumble and leap and the bells at their wrists and ankles jangle right loud as they move among the crowds. A fight breaks out near the fire and a man falls. The crowd claps and jeers. Samain is just getting started.

I am a mite afraid now, everyone is getting loose and easy. A lot of the yelling and crying out is in fun, but I reckon a lot of it is not. It's hard to tell the one from the other, but it happens every year that people are hurt, sometimes injured badly, an' so are we cats.

I stick by Duncan. Sick of waiting, he leaves Crowe's side and moves to another part of the crowd where we see Luke Harker with Charlotte and Hannah. Isla is not with them, and I wonder where she has got to. I jump up to nestle in Hannah's arm, occasionally shooting out my legs and stretching my paws. Where better could I be, to keep an eye on these people?

Luke does not bother to hide his look of boredom.

Duncan curses the man. 'Ye should at least pretend to be happy to be out with yer beloved! Why, if I had a body ye'd be sorry ye'd ever been born!'

Bairns run up and down with small fizzing sticks that burn their wee fingers. Their parents clap and chant. Here on the Royal Mile burns the biggest bonfire of them all with everyone around looking expectant and anxious.

Duncan grins at the site of Mr. Muir, who stands and waves to the wee group of Hannah, Charlotte and Luke. A young woman close beside Duncan's old apprentice has a brood of young ones hanging off her skirts.

'Aha,' cries Hannah, spotting him. 'Mr. Muir is here!' She waves to him in return.

'I see Mary King,' a shrill voice calls and everyone

looks around. Hands point in varying directions to where the legendary child may still be crying for her lost doll.

Charlotte spots the pastor and calls out to him. 'Pastor Furphy! Hullo! Over here . . . ' but her words lose themselves in the hubbub.

Jumping out of Hannah's arms, I begin a slow walk back and forth, rubbing against her ankles.

Isla's narrative

The peaceful morning spent with Charlotte and Hannah seems a long time ago. Now all is hustle and bustle so that I ponder what this evening will bring to me and to Edinburgh. Already the noise is deafening and I float higher. I am idly wondering if Duncan will ever show himself again or if he has forgotten me altogether, when I absent-mindedly fall to rubbing my ring and watch the wee light show. I do not say that it is not marvellous, but its magic is beginning to pale and it seems not to hold the promise that it previously did. Never mind! It is Samain and there is excitement all round me! I see several people I know standing in the light of the fires, their eyes afizz and at the same time watchful. Aye, I have always liked this time and travel up and down searching for my Dunc, but allowing my eyes to wander and enjoy the sights. Wee bairns scream with delight.

Belle's narrative

Watching the crowd milling about on the Royal Mile, looking for an opportunity, Sandy ambles casually toward a family group. He tries his boot on me, but I elude him and he has no more time to waste. He is too busy observing the family that stands nearby, especially the father, as he lifts a small blonde lad from his mother's arms. As he places the child on the ground, the man's jacket swings back, revealing the contents of an inner pocket. Uh-oh! Sandy steps back, his face unconcerned, his eyes on the bonfire, cheering with the rest of the crowd. After a few minutes the boy lifts its arms to its mother, crying a wee bit, and she bends to pick him up; Sandy swears silently, but then the mother gives a soft moan, putting her hand to her back. Sandy quietly steps into position and while the father is still giving the woman a concerned look, Sandy has his hand at the ready. As the man lifts the child, he loses his wallet. It all happens in a heartbeat.

'Thief!' yells the father. 'Thief!'

Everyone turns to look, even Charlotte, Hannah and Luke. Here is more excitement! I cannot keep still and stay where I am with such a chase before me and I'm off to join in the fun before they know it.

Sandy panics. He pockets the wallet and runs dodging through the crowded and intricate alleyways that he knows so well. I do my best to keep up, a poor second. The man chases after him shouting as Sandy follows a tangled rabbit warren that will come eventually to the rooms of some underground catacombs where he could disappear. Others join the chase. Constable Dundee slowly gains on him. Crowe's mesmerised face leaps out at him. Sandy hares it. I hear his laboured breathing and if his legs ache like mine with this climbing of Edinburgh's steep roads, he is in agony. The cap flies off his flaming red hair; it is the signpost to his downfall. Everywhere people block his flight. Everywhere light from blazing fires exposes and endangers him. He darts into a recessed doorway, painful lungs wheezing but he strives not to be heard. Sandy curses his luck, and this rotten Samain. He has never been caught. He bends his body and shrinks back into the shadows. I wait nearby, trying to regain my breath. The constable rounds the corner.

Isla's narrative

Och! Here is a fine thing with good-looking Scotsmen everywhere and not a Duncan Abernathy to be seen! To be sure he was never shy about showing hisself, and enjoyed a jig or a reel as much as anyone. So I ken there is some deep reason for his no-appearance – either I am not looking hard enough or he is not, though he were never a lazy bugger. I give myself up to the many distractions. See how the loon dances before the flames, inviting them to consume him. This is what the night of Samain does do to us all, the liberty to be a bit mad, to do what ye normally would shun, to take a disguise and act the fool, or to rob a wee sweetie for a bairn just too see if ye can do it, daring yerself to the mischief. Aye, there is the good side and the bad to Samain. See yon men with their collars turned up and their hats pulled low, standing in groups on the dark rim of the light from the bonfires. They are up to no good and most respectable folk are on watch for their goings on. Those men who bring their womenfolk and bairns tonight will not care to be found wanting.

I do see many other ghosts wandering about and give the nod to those I have known, very bonnie to see them it is. I ask if they have seen my Duncan but none have done so and advise me to head out to Calton Burial Ground for better information. I hope it does nay come to that, I dinna like the place! Besides I feel in my bones (do nay tell me I have none, for that is where I feel it) that he is here, nearby and whatever is about to happen will happen soon. The feeling has been welling up all day and damn me for a sinner if I do not find him this very night!

Belle's narrative

The majesty of the law turns the corner and lunges down the laneway. Constable Dundee cannot see Sandy, nor any red hair, so he slows down and finally stops in his tracks as he surveys the succession of doorways before him. I make as much noise near Sandy as my tired lungs will allow, but the constable pays me no mind. Raising his whistle to his lips Dundee blows loudly, and soon another two constables arrive at his side. He explains swiftly. Taking out their batons they move in a group of three to the first doorway. In the eerie blackness, the light cast by their lantern seems like a dim sun. A few townsmen come up behind them, eager to see the drama.

The constables find the first doorway empty. 'Come out!' they shout. Ye'll not get away!'

The robbed man curses.

Sandy cowers further down the alleyway; if he moves at all they will see him as clear as I do. He stays as still as a mouse. Footsteps echo nearby, coming closer. Many footsteps. What will they do to him? He can expect nothing good. Shrinking back, Sandy pushes with all his might against the door behind him, but it does not give. In desperation, he bursts out into the lane, running like a hare. In the ensuing chase, the constables close on him until they can grab him, bringing him to the ground and give him a wee bit extra in the way of kicks and punches for the crime of disturbing their Samain. This time I don't run; I am fagged out, but I do walk down. While kicking out with his boots, Sandy covers his face with his hands but the blows continue. He can do nothing but curl up in a ball. The constables halt to get their breath, looking at the wicked lump of humanity on the ground. At last they pull him cruelly to his feet. 'Aye, ye've had enough, he ye?' one asks, giving him another jab. 'There's plenty more of that if you're wantin' it.'

Reaching for the bulge in Sandy's pocket, the man who was robbed pulls out his own wallet.

'Your name, sir?' says Dundee.

'My name is James Savage,' he says, 'and *this* is my wallet.'

While they are sorting out these details, Sandy's chin falls forward; his chest heaves. He is too winded to speak. Two of the men pull his arms back and tie them together. As a body, they push him back along the way they came until we all emerge into the firelight. 'That's the one,' someone in the crowd cries. 'Look at that hair.'

Sandy flinches, but lifts his head boldly so that his red hair catches the wind and the light. 'Be damned, the lot of ye,' he roars at them all. He is a sight -- with his back bent forward and his head pulled back he forms the shape of an S, all be it a sight of misery.

The crowd escorts him back to the site where Mr. Savage rejoins his family.

'Aye, that's him,' says the wife who looks wild, shaking her fist at Sandy as though she would like to add her own slap to the belting he has had.

Sandy looks away and sees Crowe and Tom on the fringes of the crowd. Once more he attempts to stand tall, but he cannot straighten his back after the beating he has taken. Constable Dundee pushes him roughly at this deputies, who march him off in the direction of the watch house. Dundee will remain. Aye the man is brick – he has been here, there and everywhere this night. The constable will stay but now I should l go back to my charges.

Leaving Crowe to run up to the road, Tom halts

right in Sandy's path as the beaten man, willing himself on, approaches. Summoning all his reserves, Sandy winks at Tom, who looks back helplessly before turning his head to look at Crowe in the distance, thin but so solid a figure that he resembles a human brick wall.

Tom opens his mouth and wails like a scalded cat. I sit by his feet; he needs me and for the moment I cannot leave him.

Crowe calls and beckons, but Tom does not return. No, he runs off, dodging through the crowd, moving at random, lost in the darkness, sobbing like a child. Crowe lets him go, knowing that Tom is undone by the speed and violence of events, by the wild excitement of Samain and by his own feeble mind. Keeping his eyes down, and his movements small, Crowe heads for the pub. And now I really *must* get back to Charlotte and Hannah!

Isla's narrative

I make my way idly up the Royal Mile when from my elevated vantage point I see people ahead, people that could be Charlotte and Hannah, except that they are well away from the action. What are they doing in such an out of the way place? Belle is with them and there! There is something near them, something of Duncan's shape and size. Could this be it? I lunge forward, praying hard – Och! If I still had a heart people for miles about would hear it beating strong.

Belle's narrative

Just as I turn away from watching this moment when Tom and Crowe are going their separate ways, I stagger under the heavy weight of Samain coming down and I am still not there with Charlotte and Hannah. Because unexpectedly, my whole being is alive with a new direction, to go from here and get, as fast as I can, to the Royal Infirmary. I hate to do so but there is a dreadful urgency about this knowledge and I fear that I ken what it does mean. I merge into the darkness, padding on silent paws. I will try to be back before they even know I am gone. Perhaps when I return Isla will be with Duncan. I hope so, because I am being pushed on my way, by what force I dinna know, towards the Royal Infirmary.

Lying in the bed next to Flora, in the grey and gloomy room, the old lady snores in a regular rhythm. I am astounded that here is all the loud mayhem of Samain and still she snores. Even from my vantage point on Flora's bed, I find the great intermittent noises and cries that come from outside very frightening. The snoring has been Flora's constant companion, and I suppose she does not notice it any longer but it seems over-loud to me. Flora's thin body strains against the covers, twisting this way and that so she does not miss a detail of the action outside the windows. Flora is so excited that her eyes, as black as coal against her pale skin, seem even larger and brighter than usual. 'Here is a grand Samain, my Flo,' says her

Da, who stands at the end of her bed, watching her as she watches the fires. When she turns to him, he shifts his gaze to the window.

'Aye, faither, grand,' she speaks carefully, in a whisper, so that she does not cough.

The lights of the fire flicker through the windows; they dance along the interior walls. Shadows of people and bursts of brightness move there, plain to see. Flora doesn't know whether to look inside or out; she has never been so close to the excitement. I feel her wee heart thumping as if she had run a race.

Outside, the fires are startlingly brilliant against a pitch-black sky. Flora's whole face is lit from within. Her skin glows and her eyes burn; all of her energy is concentrated in those two shining stars. It seems to me that she is nothing but eyes. Her gaze shifts constantly from the spectacle outside to the figure of her faither and on to the reflections dancing on the wall behind him, then back to the window and round again.

Dr. Walters hurries down the aisle to join them. Several other patients who have been woken by the noise stare out the windows, half entertained and half fearful. Some know they are close to death and that it is Samain. A child's shriek pierces the air and they all turn their heads but there is nothing to see.

'I expect injuries tonight,' says the doctor. 'There are always burns on Samain.' Two men scuffle outside the window so close that even the glass rattles; locked in tense embrace the men move out of view. 'And fights,' he adds with a shake of his head.

Frightened, Flora turns to her faither, but he gives her a wink and a grin and she goes back to watching the window.

A commotion of shouts at the door draws all eyes, and two men run in, one with burns to his arms; the patients shrink away at the smell of burnt flesh. Dr. Walters rushes over to the new arrivals.

But something else has happened: the feeling of otherworldliness has settled over us all and the blanket of dread is here. I leap down to the floor and wait for whatever may happen.

Daniel Ferguson turns back to his wee daughter and his breath stops.

The blazing figure of his wife, Erin, hovers over the bed as Flora's lifeless body settles to stillness.

Daniel reaches out instinctively to her, his mouth open in a strangled cry.

Erin, gazing at him steadily, gently gathers the child into her arms.

His little Flora looks him full in the face as she is lifted into her mother's arms. Her huge eyes plead with him. Erin holds her child tight against her as, waving her hand, she beckons her husband.

Daniel staggers forward. His breaking heart jolts through its final beat. Erin's eyes lightning-bolt into his and, as his body topples forward onto the floor, his spirit rushes to embrace them. I look all around, but no one except me has noticed. There is no commotion, even with Daniel's body lying there. Flora's body lays on the bed, as it always has. I would like to say goodbye, but they are gone and I've no wish to stay, now, without them. And this time I *will* get back to Charlotte and Hannah, come hell or high water.

I am out of breath but at least I am back, when I see a dark form steal up beside Luke. 'Can I speak to you for a moment, Mr. Harker? In private like?' He virtually hisses the words.

The man wears his old suit with a sloppy but knowing air and his smile is smug. Luke frowns at the intrusion but when he turns and sees the man's face, his expression changes. Nodding to the stranger, he turns to Charlotte and says abruptly, 'I'll be back directly, my dear,' and walks off before she can reply.

'What is this?' says Duncan as he overhears this low exchange. Straightening his unsubstantial body, he exclaims to me, 'Ah, something is about to be revealed, some skulduggery, I'll wager, my Belle. Be ready when I say.'

Charlotte looks surprised that Luke should leave her thus, in the middle of the crowd and at night on Samain. She turns to Hannah who stares with disapproval at his retreating back.

'It is not right of him to go off like that,' Hannah says, mirroring Charlotte's thoughts. 'The night is not safe.' Charlotte nods and looks disconcerted, but quickly smiles as though nothing is wrong.

Across the way, Mr. Muir looks as though he is worried and would like to come over if his nieces and nephews would just stop dashing here and there like a brood of month-old puppies.

'I'm sorry, chick,' Hannah yawns, 'but I am so tired I think I will go home to bed when Mr. Harker comes back.'

'And I think I will come wi' ye,' Charlotte says. 'I have had enough.'

'Good lass!' exclaims Duncan. 'Tell the man to go boil his head!'

I commence a great mewing and making a fine feline fuss. Charlotte bends down and rubs her hand along my spine and around my head, folding down my ears; I press back against her hand, purring. She is always gentle. The crackling bonfire, alive with small explosions, propels a stray spark too close for liking and I spring away with a sharp wail. Hannah and Charlotte cry out.

'Good, Belle, good! Ah, this is it. Let us go and listen to yon villains. We must bring Hannah and Charlotte too!' Duncan speaks coaxingly, 'Come on Belle, come on.' He twiddles his fingers and beckons. I stare at him. Of course I am coming, but I love it when people perform this strange palaver and let it go on for a moment. Nevertheless, this is serious and I go to him. We are off! As Duncan follows Luke, I follow Duncan; he goes slowly up the lane, all the time making sure Charlotte and Hannah are behind us. I sound as pitiful as I can so that they keep following me. They keep calling out, 'come along, Belle, come home with us.' Och, they are good-hearted; they too have heard the black tales of cats being caught and burned up in the bonfires of Samain. But I canna go back; they must come with me.

'Come on Belle, my fine lady,' Duncan carols almost at the same time as the others, as if they were in competition. And of course it is him that I follow and on we go; each time he takes a step I take four. Charlotte and Hannah follow me. Moving further away from the crowd, we find ourselves in a lane where light and sound is muted. I keep mewing so that Hannah and Charlotte know I am there and I lead them on until we come to a dim corner; it is too dark to see more than a couple of yards ahead but I can smell better than any of them and I know we are close to Luke and the stranger. In a moment we hear deep male voices, subdued but clear enough; however, I cannot make out any words and doubt anyone else can.

'That sounds a bit like Luke's voice,' Charlotte whispers, shivering. 'I'm not certain though. Should we move closer?' She looks at Hannah who shrugs. Here they are far from the fires, and the darkness is oppressive; they move closer together and Hannah grips Charlotte's arm in her own, but they do not move forward. Beside me I sense the protective feelings of Duncan moving, flooding toward his granddaughter.

And it is at this moment, while Duncan is so concentrated on the scene before him, that I see the faint figure of Isla approaching.

And here is the real Samain, arriving with a cold

rush that overtakes the town and all that surrounds it. This night has already seen much happen, all with the dead walking among us, for good or ill. The blanket of Samain falls; the spirits rejoice.

'Och, come closer!' Duncan cries to Charlotte and Hannah. 'Come and hear what a rogue yon Luke is!' I agree, for why else would Luke remove himself so far away from them, and speak so low? Trying to hear what is said, Duncan falls to absent-mindedly rubbing his thumb over his wedding ring. Suddenly he goes fuzzy around the edges, begins to waver and fade, and with a terrible tearing sound he is ripped from where he is and flung with desperate force into the ether. I let fly a scream to the confusion of those around me. I look expectantly upward but can see nothing and am wondering what to do when I feel a mad tingle run down my spine.

Isla's narrative

There is a sudden massive outpouring of light, huge vibrating balls of flame that dwarf the usual sparks. A powerful jolt pushes me forward. I find myself propelled out into the crowded lanes, like a small fish entering into a great school of herrings. I know this is it. My chance. All doubts gone, I search for Duncan, knowing that somewhere in this place, he is looking for me. My whole being strains forward. Suddenly a positive blizzard of sparks engulfs me. It is a great joining of fireworks, a supreme razzle dazzle and then I am in his arms; at last my man is here. I shake and sob with relief. Aye, it is he; he is here, we are together. Inside the wild circle of sparks that surround us, we glow as one entity. In a tiny slice of time, everything is well again.

We do not speak but join our ghostly hands. The two rings touch in another glorious burst of light. I have never seen such a heavenly glow.

* * *

We are pulled upward. We soar unevenly along the lanes, over the bonfires, past the lighted windows and the blazing torches, as below us chaos rules. I sense there is some job to be done, some desperate situation we need to remedy. Despite the sudden fact of our reunion after so long, it seems that there is no time to rejoice; we must act. We fly. I don't even have a chance to ask Duncan what is going on; I am oppressed by a sense of urgency. Beneath us Luke Harker and another man come into sight. Before we get to them, we each, at the same exact moment, spy Belle, a wee distance away from the crowds. Near her stand Hannah and Charlotte, just before the corner of an old building, it's summer window boxes now barren. Luke and his companion are on the other side, deep in conversation. Clutching each other, Duncan and I descend in a whirlwind, wildly exhilarated and laughing like children as we come to a stop.

Belle is momentarily disconcerted and caterwauls like a she-devil as she spies Duncan, then me; her face has a knowing look if a cat can have such a thing. Per-

haps it is all the Samain in her this night. Our exhilaration drains away.

Dunc calls to her and she takes a half step back. The movement is just enough for Hannah to spot her hindquarters in the dim light.

'Come Belle, time to go home,' Hannah calls. She twiddles her fingers, 'come here now, ye wee daftie,' she whispers, leaning forward, stretching out her hand.

Belle purrs and steps away, moving up the lane toward Luke and the stranger; Charlotte and Hannah follow Belle. Duncan and I hover over the two men, chirruping softly to Belle. Charlotte must come closer; she must be near enough to hear what they say.

In the murmur of the men's talk, the stranger raises his voice. 'And what about Leanne?' he asks. 'She has been waiting long enough. She's my sister, for God's sake, and YOUR WIFE!' Luke's voice rumbles in consternation, but the damning words have been let loose into the world and Charlotte, having rounded the corner in her search for Belle, has heard them. In shock, she falls. A wicked crack sounds as her head hits the stone cobbles. Hannah cries out at the sight of the bright red blood. Luke and turn at the same moment toward the sound. The colour drains from their faces.

Belle runs at Luke, jumping up and tearing at his face, clawing it so that the blood flows. Duncan and I, horrified at Charlotte's state, gaze at the rare mess we have made. With a swift movement, the stranger disappears into the darkness.

Hannah drops to her knees, cradling Charlotte's

head in her arms. 'Help!' she screams. 'Help!' But we cannot help. Her hands turn red, and she screams again, a wild forlorn wail. She looks madly around. There is only Luke, still scuffling with Belle and he is losing the battle. The cat smothers his face, her claws tearing at his scalp. He is buried in fur and teeth.

Luke's sudden confusion, as he curses violently from pain and fear, prevents him from moving. He cannot get to Charlotte; nor can he run away. Belle bats him around the head, scratching him with her needle claws and biting where she can.

'Here! Somebody, help me!' Hannah yells again. To Charlotte she whispers, 'Come on my bonny one. Help is coming.'

Charlotte eyes are closed; blood flows down over them. She lets out a low moan. Hannah holds her tighter.

Sharp steps sound and a familiar voice shouts, 'Hannah, what is it? What's happened?' Suddenly John Muir is beside them, his appalled face deathly pale. He quickly lifts Charlotte, and runs quickly back toward the lights, heading for the Royal Infirmary with Hannah close on his heels. Bright red blood drips onto the cobbles as they rush onward and Constable Dundee races up to join them.

Duncan and I fly anxiously after the strange procession. 'What is the harvest to be?' he asks. 'What have I done? Me and my interfering?' What indeed? I wonder. My joy has turned to fear, my certainty to bewilderment. We are to blame; that much is certain. But what of Charlotte and her poor head?

I am beside myself with worry. Och! How I wish to be alive now and able to help, but I can only watch as Muir tenderly lays Charlotte on a bed; the sudden loss of blood has made her look as white as the sheets around her. Dr. Walters moves quickly to her side, elevates her head and examines her wound. The corners of his mouth turn down as Charlotte lets out a moan but he must tightly secure a bandage masking her face. While Hannah holds her hand, Muir paces.

'Press here,' he says to Hannah. 'She may cry out but you must press hard until I return.'

Hannah presses.

'And me, doctor, what can I do?' Muir cries.

'Keep watch, man. Let no one near,' says Walters, and is gone.

During all the long wait, and even though Charlotte does groan at one point, Hannah doesn't lessen the pressure, stoutly keeping it strong even as she sees lines of pain tighten around Charlotte's closed eyes. I can feel her and young Muir willing the doctor to come back; I feel the same and cannot settle until he returns with a tray of instruments. Lifting Charlotte's head and pinching her nose, Walters pours a small vial of liquid into her mouth and pushes up her jaw. She swallows and falls back. In a moment her face relaxes; we hear no more moaning.

Duncan and I hold each other close. A sense of horror and blame burns in us; we don't know what will happen. We canna take our eyes off our Charlotte, whose pale blank face frightens and appals us. Our longed-for reunion has faded in importance. We are mute.

'Charlotte!' Luke Harker runs into the large ward, disturbing the relative quiet. The scratches all around his face and head are seeping blood. He is a horrid sight; all bloody and raw, his fine coat stained a dark burgundy. Looking about him he spots Hannah, then Muir and seeming blind to the look of abhorrence on their faces, his eyes move quickly on to Charlotte. For all the villainy he has done, he still seems shocked at the state of her. The crimson of her wound sets off the extreme pallor of her dear face, made worse by the closed eyelids and unnatural stillness.

John Muir with something like ferocity in her eyes, steps forward, blocking Luke's way. Dr. Walters turns to Luke abruptly, saying, 'Go to the other room, young man. Someone will see to your injuries.'

Muir shoves him back. Luke gapes at him, still dazed. The doctor signals to Constable Dundee who hovers close to Charlotte. Taking him firmly by the arm and pulling him away, the constable seems glad to remove him. No doubt he has much work still before him on this night of nights.

'What? Why?' Luke gasps. 'Charlotte!' Luke calls again. 'It's me, Luke.'

Then he is gone and the room is quiet. I am glad. I hate the sight of that man and despise his lying ways.

Getting straight to work, Dr. Walters swabs Charlotte's wounds with a tincture of alcohol that causes *the flow of blood to slow down. The man is a marvel. He sets out his stall and sews together the pale skin, as tidy as a woman putting together a dress. The stitches stand out darkly on Charlotte's forehead as the doctor begins to bandage it neatly. Then he turns to Hannah and Muir.*

'Ye'll stay with her?' he asks.

They nod shakily. 'Aye, we'll be here.'

Thank God they are stout! With neither Duncan nor I able to help, our feelings of guilt and frustration drown us. We have caused this and I hope that the good Lord will forgive our meddling. Now we must watch closely and be sure that no more harm is done.

Hannah carefully loosens Charlotte's heather dress, and washes the bloodied area — neck, ears and shoulders — cooing softly, calling her 'angel'. She covers her with a warm quilt, tucking her in and looking on with worry. We see her lips moving. Aye, she is a good woman, Hannah. Muir brings a chair and places it beside the bed and Hannah sighs before sinking into it, tired and looking around her.

'Thank ee, John,' she says automatically. 'And where is Belle?' she asks softly, but Belle has vanished, probably headed for home and comfort, as Hannah would if things were otherwise. Our wise tabby will find her way back and get in through her own secret entry. Duncan and I are still a 'watching, beginning to feel a mite calmer now. The wound is dressed and Charlotte looks as if she is sleeping, but we are all frightened by the chance of an infection. Muir has found another chair

and looking stern, keeps watch at the bedside. He looks as if he would like to take Charlotte's other hand in his own.

Another Samain is beginning to slow down; the commotion outside the Infirmary gradually dies away. The fires have burned low, becoming beds of bright embers, warming the few people still outside. Most of the revellers are heading for home. Others, many with burns to the hands, come to the Infirmary, keeping the ward busy. Dr. Walters moves from bed to bed, checking on each case, occasionally looking over at Charlotte. She is in good hands.

Finally, I look away from the sleeping Charlotte, a dozing Hannah and a vigilant John so that I may set my gaze on Duncan.

'Well,' says I. 'An, ye finally remembered ye had a wife after all.'

'An' ye a husband. Where have ye been all this time?' Duncan replies.

'Och! I wish ye had a body so I could poke ye in the ribs, ma wee mannie.' Aye, now the worst of the worry is over it feels grand to have him back. But we have been too rash, caused trouble for the wee chick. And yet . . . at least now she knows about that Luke Harker and the villain that he be. And I am glad of it, even as I am beset by guilt.

'Do ye think she will recover?' I say to Duncan, worried by the blood on her face that we can see in the bursts of light, and her erratically pulsing veins. So ill, so ill.

1 November

Belle's narrative

My good God, what a night! I've been home in Charlotte's bed a wee while now and still I can hear the wild shouts and goings on and am confident it will go on till the morning light makes all look stale and sad. After I was sure that Charlotte was safe and sleeping peacefully I came back but it is lonely here with no one about. I will sleep in time, and all with one eye open. The dark sky is ribboned with a red glow and the wind still howls. How glad I am to be quiet! Now I have time to reflect and think of poor Flora and her da, and of that daftie Tom, and how he escaped a fate like Sandy's. It seems as if I have been enough time at the Royal Infirmary, but I will be back there soon to check on my remaining charges. I'll also have a look at the villain Luke, as it seems I did not scratch him hard enough last night. I would like to see him right criss-crossed with red welts.

Isla's narrative

It is the next morning, when Duncan and I waft into the light of the hospital ward. Charlotte is sitting up in bed and looking around her with an air of being lost.

'There she is, our chick, well rid of that idiot,' says

Dunc. 'Is she better, do you think? But how sad she seems. I should like to horse whip that fine dandy for what he's done to her.'

'A very improper thought for a spirit,' says I. 'Tut, tut.'

'A very proper thought, I say,' Duncan twinkles. 'It is only justice.'

With slow but steady hands, Charlotte eats her oats and milk. Her eyes, blacker than obsidian, display the same dull shine as the dark stone. Those eyes have changed, lost their bright sparkle. But it is early days.

Sitting at her bedside, Hannah murmurs softly to her from time to time.

'I'm sure it is all for the best,' she says. 'Ye had a near escape, I fear. Now, ye must rest and get better.'

'Aye,' says Muir, from his place at the door.

'Aye.' Charlotte can hardly speak; her face is horribly bruised. Eating must be hard, too, because she puts down her spoon slowly without finishing her food, and she picks up the cup of tea with a shaking hand. Taking a sip, she lays her head back on the pillow. Even if she could speak more comfortably I think that she could have no real talk in her. Why would she want to speak about such betrayal? What words could she find?

Our Belle steps grandly into the room and plants a deep look on Duncan and me. Mayhap she feels as guilty as we two.

Duncan puts his finger on his lips. 'Well done last night,' he whispers.

'Ah, an here comes Belle to say hello,' cries Muir. 'She gets about the town, does she not?'

'Aye, that she does. Here Belle,' Charlotte says weakly, patting the blanket that covers her. Leaping smoothly onto the bed, Belle settles down in the warm crook of Charlotte's arm, gazing at Hannah for a brief moment before closing her eyes. With Charlotte weakly stroking her fur, Belle purrs with that comforting rhythm that vibrates straight into yer blood. 'Ye led us a merry chase last night, did ye not,' Charlotte whispers into her small furry ear. 'And not at all do ye seem to care.' Stretching and yawning, Belle shows us her sharp tiny teeth that give a hint of her true steel, and her rough rasping tongue that reminds us that she is a wild animal at heart. She settles back and dozes, giving her human the warmth and companionship of her resting body.

'I hope ye may be coming home today,' Hannah says. 'It seems Dr. Walters usually comes through here in the morning and he will let us know.' She lapses into silence, for Charlotte has shut her eyes.

While Charlotte rests, her pale face beset by the rich dark hair, her closed eyes and the terrible stillness of her, I try to see her through Muir's eyes. He goes toward her directly. I feel for him; all this time he has been waiting, thinking he had no chance while Luke Harker was about, and now that Luke is discovered for the villain that he is, poor Charlotte is injured and out of Muir's reach again.

'Ye look a sight brighter than ye did last night,' he says.

'Och, ye be a fine liar, John Muir. Come closer so I can see ye – my eyes are a wee bit fuzzy,' Charlotte says.

Mr. Muir comes right up to the bed; his eyes crinkle as he gets close enough to have a good look at Charlotte. She does not look at all like her bonny self. Half of her face is covered by grazing and bruises from where she fell onto the uneven cobbled lane way; a black eye is swollen tight shut. Higher up near her temple is a bandage of such pure whiteness it hurts the eyes to look at it. Skin of a terrible pallor shows on the other half of her face. Hannah stands and says she will go 'stretch her legs'.

Opening her eyes a wee bit wider, Charlotte gives Mr. Muir a half smile of welcome. How good it is to see that smile, twisted though it is. She has been through a lot, poor mite. 'I must thank ye for yer help last night, Mr Muir. My face must be all the colours of the rainbow. They will not let me have a mirror,' she says softly.

'Och, it's not so bad. Give it a few days. Ye are still a beauty, I dare say. But how are you feeling, Miss Charlotte? That is the important thing.' Mr. Muir's words rush together without giving her a second to answer him. 'It was a terrible accident ye had last night, and I'm relieved to see ye awake, at the least, though ye are verra sore and sorry looking.' He remains on his feet, his expression an open book as it changes back and forth between a fear that he may not be welcome and an urgent desire to stay. 'Here, I have found ye a wee bit of arnica for the bruises.' He produces a small packet from his coat and offers it.

Belle lifts her head and looks a bold question into his eyes. Aha!

'I am mending, Mr. Muir,' murmurs Charlotte. 'I thank ye for the arnica; have ye been here all night then?'

'Och aye, of course I could not leave ye. But I'll be in the shop on time, to be sure.'

'Aye, I'll be fine, the doctor tells me,' Charlotte says slowly. 'It will just take a few days to heal. I can bear it.'

Hannah returns with a cup of tea that she offers to Mr. Muir. He takes it, but his hand is shaking a wee bit and the cup rattles on the saucer. Embarrassed, he puts the cup down carefully. 'Ye'll be wanting to rest, I fear, and I must be away. Hannah will be by ye.'

'Thank ye, Mr. Muir. I'll be home as soon as I can. I've no desire to stay in this dreary place.' Charlotte begins to yawn but does not; I ken she discovers her bruises are better undisturbed. 'Good-bye.'

'Good-bye. Send if ye need anything, anything at all.'

As Mr. Muir walks away, Charlotte turns to Hannah. 'Ah, Hannah, I wish for nothing so much as to sleep and forget and sleep again.'

'Go on and close your eyes, chick. I'll stay here beside ye and read my bible until the doctor comes. Don't worry.' Hannah tucks her in, covering up her cold hands, and her shoulders right up to her chin, leaving *only Charlotte's discoloured face, next to Belle's stripey one, peeking out above the covers.*

So it seems that our lassie is going to be fine. She will not marry that scoundrel, and she will go home again with Hannah to care for her. And Muir it seems. But we are still at fault and I don't want to forget what we did, just because things have turned out well. Soon we will be called away and we will have to answer for our sins, aye.

14 November

Belle's narrative

In the morning, the pearly sky peels back its layers, revealing streaks of blue and pink that shimmer in peaceful quietude. See what a poet I can be! I'll guess ye did not think I had it in me. Aye, but it is naught save a sad morning for some.

'Ian Alexander McCrae, known as Sandy McCrae, it is alleged that on the night of the 31st October 1833, you did pick the pocket of Mr. James Savage, merchant of this town; thereby you are charged with theft. What do you plead?'

This is a place I rarely come to; it's not a friendly place by miles. Besides, I do not think they like me at the court. Judge Hart's condemnatory tone, his forbidding appearance half-hidden by black robes and a fair wig, makes me uneasy and makes Sandy seethe with both despair and anger he dares not show. Thoroughly kicked and beaten the night before, he is aware that Hart is unlikely ever to have faced hardship, let alone destitution. The judge looks at him out of brittle eyes that harbour a dark aspect of ill will. Sandy knows that he is already condemned.

Stretching out behind Sandy, a dishevelled line of Samain miscreants wait in a long and forbidding room lined with narrow windows and dark wood. Large empty spaces of chill air make them shiver. The light is so dim that candles are lit even in daytime. The judge sits at a high imposing desk, with officers on either side. I do nay like Sandy, but somehow I like the judge even less.

'Not guilty, Your Honour,' Sandy says.

'On what grounds?'

'It was nay me; it must have been another.'

Judge Hart fixes him wearily with his cruel eyes.

'All witnesses, including the aggrieved party, identify you as the man. I feel I am ready and informed to pronounce sentence. You are to be transported to Van Dieman's Land with seven years hard labour.' He nods to the bailiff. 'Take him away. Ye will spend your time in gaol until the next ship is ready to leave.'

A lonely figure, Sandy spots Tom, his mouth hanging open, his eyes anxious and broken, at the back of the court. Though not resisting as the bailiff leads him away, he holds his head high, and looks defiance at all. He roars, 'May ye all rot that live in this accursed city of Edinburgh. I damn ye all to hell!' He shakes with rage and powerlessness. 'A man canna live in such a torment as this.'

Stepping back, Tom follows the desolate man as he leaves the courtroom. Outside, Tom stops, turns and starts off again in another direction. I follow Tom; I know where he is going. There is nowhere but the pub on a cold and windy day such as this. And there Crowe sits with his back to the window, drinking his pint and letting his muddy eyes wander around to where a few men play cards or dominoes. I know the stories of all these men, but that is for another tale. Sandy, Crowe knows, is gone for good, to be hanged or transported; there will be no other outcome. I suppose that Sandy livened things up a bit, though I think that Crowe hated him right through. He's always hated him, ever since the day Sandy had recruited him (and later Tom) straight from the orphanage, and seduced him into a poor excuse for a life.

Sitting down opposite Crowe while I curl myself up by the fire, Tom says, 'Seven years in Van Dieman's Land.' He utters the words with a shudder. 'He were lucky; there were two hangings this morning. It were old Black Hart on the bench.'

Crowe gestures to the barman to bring a dram for Tom.

'Aye, but he was nay a good man, Tom. Remember how he laughed at ye and tricked ye.'

Tom ignores him. Having given his news, he has little else to say; unlike Sandy, he drops his head. 'He were one of us, Crowe.'

'Och, I know! He nay had a chance with that old bastard. Have yer drink, Tom, and do not think on it. It is done now.'

Tom drinks and holds out his mug for another.

When Crowe finishes filling their mugs, Tom lifts his eyes; the intensity in them makes Crowe flinch. He leans back against the wall, watching Tom quickly finish his dram and pour another. 'What is it, man? Do ye miss the wee bugger? Was he such a braw friend to ye?'

'He were one of us. It's wrong. He never hurt nobody. He picked a pocket, that's all.' Tom turns his face to the window. 'I dinna want him to go to Van Dieman's Land, nay, I do not.'

'It is a fearsome place, they say, aye, but Sandy will be all right. Ye know how strong he is. Do ye no remember how he fought in that lane with three men and got away complete?'

'Aye.' Tom purses his lips. His forehead wrinkles and he looks owlish. 'I know.'

Crowe turns to look out the small window at the cold and windy outdoors. The man has a hard row to hoe. Occasionally, when someone passes under the bare branches of the large oak tree opposite, he heaves up a sigh.

Time for me to go.

Isla's narrative

Here is a wild sight for such as us. Duncan and I sit to-

gether, resting on our own tombstones as we wait for what will come. Down in the back blocks of the Calton Burial Ground the spirits have had their fun. Drunk on their antics of Samain and the terror of those that they scared, they brag and swagger; but they will stay here, lost for another year, the poor wee fools. I dinna care how they howl at the passers by and at the moon, or how eagerly they wait for people to die, for I am well, even as the cold wind rises.

'It seems our Charlotte is going to be alright, Duncan, my man,' I say. 'The roses are coming back into her cheeks; did ye not see her smile today without a bit of sadness?'

'Aye, I know it; she will recover, and she is just a wee bit the wiser now. Those villains are behind bars for their wicked deeds. They could nay have got a sentence long enough for my liking.'

'Nay, nor mine.'

'And I am glad to see my old apprentice is takng such good care of her.'

'Aye, a much better man he is!'

Calton is an eerie sight. The tombstones are a cold shade of blue, throwing blue-black shadows on the ground. The shifting of the clouds allows a grand shine of moonlight to drift over the graves in quick jerky movements. A show for us.

'I think it may be our time to go,' says Duncan. 'At least, it must be mine; I have been waiting so long, waiting for ye, my bonny, that I think my time is up.'

'Aye. Well, you've left me once but ye'll no be going

anywhere without me again.' I lift my hand with its plain gold ring to rest on his. 'Are ye ready?' We have one last visit to make.

Downstairs, John Muir has made up his bed to be nearby while Charlotte recovers and Hannah is in her bed on the landing, with the curtain drawn. Charlotte, lying still next to Belle in her bed above the shop, smiles in her sleep. I know that she has heard that Charels and Luke have been sentenced, for Hannah has gone every day to the court. When our two ghostly figures drift into the bedroom, a light tingle runs through her young body, waking her. Sitting up and sliding my old engagement ring off her finger, she stares into the heart of the darkly glowing jewel, her thoughts already leaving Luke and the doings of Samain behind, and looking forward to Hogmanay and the good times she and Hannah and Mr. Muir may share. After her betrayal by Luke, Muir has risen high in her estimation, and they often share a word and a laugh. She carefully places the ring on her bedside table, lets her head drop back onto the pillow and quite soon she falls into her dreams once more. Reassured by what we see, we will be able to return from whence we came, knowing that she is coming to peace.

Resting in Charlotte's arms, Belle regards us for a moment with her magic eyes . . . and winks! — making me wonder how much she knows, how much of her life is here and how much is in that unknowable place.

Duncan nods. We entwine our ghostly fingers and in that moment of union we look to the heavens. The sky opens, showing bright depths that were dark just a mo-

ment before. Our rings touch. In the blizzard of sparks that follows a new wind begins to swirl, lifting us off the ground. We cling fast to each other and rise, borne ever higher by the whirlwind. My wonder runs riot even as my man laughs at me. But I care not what lies ahead, now that Dunc is in my arms again.

About the Author

Born in Connecticut, PJ Johnson moved to Perth, Western Australia at the age of 18. With an enduring love for stories of action and adventure, ghosts, Druids, characters that encompass both good and evil, and in the words of Edgar Allan Poe, tales of mystery and imagination, PJ entered the writing world with great enthusiasm. Isla Rising is PJ's first book but she has a long association with literary circles through editing, publishing and writing poetry. With undeniable flair, and a mind for humour, PJ's style of alternating the voices of Isla and her cat Belle allows us to see the unreal, fathom the arcane and laugh and cry at the habits of the living and the dead.

PJ has given us a remarkable book following in the footsteps of authors Russell Hoban and Garth Stein.

Acknowledgments

This is the fun part. There are many people involved in the coming together of a book and it is a pleasure to have this chance to mention them all. It must be every thankers nightmare that they may inadvertently leave someone out and although I've checked my list thankees as they appear here over and over again, I want you to know that if your name should be here and is not, I still thank you in my heart.

First of all, many thanks to Angel Writer Liana Joy Christensen, who encouraged me to put fingers to keyboard and eventually birth a red and puking baby; to editor extraordinaire Michèle Drouart, who took this mewling baby and fed and burped and changed her until she was in a state fit to unleash on an unsuspecting world; to Julie-Ann Harper and the Pickawoowoo Publishing Group and to Ingram Spark/Lightning Source for helping her take her first steps. And for the fabulously Gothic cover, a million thanks to Laila Savolainen.

The whole world of writing, literature, the innumerable books I've read, and most of all the thriving writing community of Western Australia, have been an inspiration. In particular I'd like to thank all those involved in the Creative Writing Program at Curtin University; those involved with the late great *dotdotdash* magazine; friends in the Swans Writing Group; and everyone in the Fellowship of Australian Writers Western Australia, especially the late Trisha Kotai-Ewers.

Many appreciative cheers and yippees to Jo Clarke for allowing me space to write in her beautiful Tea Tree Cottage, to Lisa Litjens for our Wednesday morning coffee and writing sessions, to Colin Young for his copy edit, and to Horst Kornberger for the inspirational writing courses and his wonderful book *Story Medicine*.

Finally to my family and many non-writing friends whose good humour and fellowship I value so highly, to Ian for much love, support and encouragement and always bringing me back to earth, and most of all to Jessie and Sam, for all the times that were, I thank you.